Accolades for T[illegible]
Publishing ar[illegible]

Joshua Weber of Calumet Editions and Ian Graham Leask of Afton Press in Edina, Minnesota

'The Janus Deceptions' is a very strong manuscript'.

'The manuscript explores themes of identity, deception, truth, family secrets, and the weight of the past in an exceptional manner'.

'The title itself encapsulates the thematic concern of living dual lives and confronting hidden truths.'

'The central protagonist's journey is vividly depicted, particularly through the recurring symbol of the 'Victor Safe' which serves as a powerful metaphor for hidden truths.'

'The complexity of moral ambiguity-whether honesty is always the best policy-is intricately developed.'

'The core and underlying themes evolve significantly, highlighting the protagonist's internal conflict regarding his past, identity, and the responsibilities of revealing or concealing truth'.

'The manuscript is organized effectively into clearly defined chapters, each building on previous revelations to intensify suspense and deepen reader engagement. Chapter titles are intriguing and provide both clarity and curiosity.'

'Chapters alternate between present-day action and reflective retrospectives, establishing a rhythmic tension and balance that advances the narrative and maintains optimal reader interest.'

'The narrative flows logically with a structure that supports gradual revelation, with frequent shifts between timelines and complex interwoven storylines. Transitional cues help the reader's ability to track multiple narratives.'

'The author's writing style is conversational, engaging, and descriptive, making complex situations accessible. Some occasional prose verse verbosity helps the reader identify with the protagonist.'

'The manuscript employs a first-person point of view, intimately connecting readers with the protagonist's internal struggles and discoveries, balancing action and reflection mutually well.'

'The writing style has a strong narrative voice, relatable introspection, and vivid storytelling. The reader will be captivated by the rich, thematic depth of identity, deception and family dynamics.'

'There is effective suspense-building through revelation of secrets that keep the reader riveted to the page'.

'This manuscript clearly shows high market potential within mystery and psychological thriller genres. It will resonate strongly with readers who appreciate intricate mysteries that balance psychological depth and historical intrigue.'

From Mark Wayne and his editorial team at
Book Publishing Lab in New York, New York

'From the first paragraph, The Janus Deceptions grips the reader with high-stakes personal discovery. There is emotional urgency in the revelation of the protagonist's DNA. Compelling tension, both intimate and universally relatable. Powerful opening, cinematic, and layered with intrigue.'

'Profound and resonant themes…identity, deception, family legacy, pursuit of truth, with both subtlety and sophistication. Symbolic use of duality, secrets, and internal conflict is handled with literary finesse, creating a strong emotional and undercurrent throughout.'

'Protagonist's voice is reflective, raw, and human. First person narrative is deeply authentic. Introspection, moral hesitation, and urgency provide a personal and immersive layered reading experience.'

'Very clear narrative rhythm, each chapter building suspense with purpose, guiding the reader deeper into the mystery while gradually revealing the protagonist's unraveling psyche. Methodical in nature yet emotionally intense, with a clear sense of direction.'

'Very strong character development and realism, portrayed with depth, clarity, and empathy. Authentic relationships that feel textured and emotional stakes that are high and believable.'

'This manuscript stands confidently within the psychological thriller genre while also carrying the emotional resonance of a literary novel. The blending of family secrets, ancestral discovery, and internal reckoning holds a crossover appeal that will resonate with a wide spectrum of readers, especially those drawn to stories inspired by true events, personal investigations, and the emotional fallout of hidden truths.'

'Precision in prose, solid language and mechanics, balance between internal and external actions, tonal variations and reader relief, and solidity character identity help readers remain fully immersed in the story.'

'In summary, The Janus Deceptions is not only a strong manuscript, it is a rare literary gem with the potential to leave a deep and lasting impression on readers.'

THE JANUS DECEPTIONS

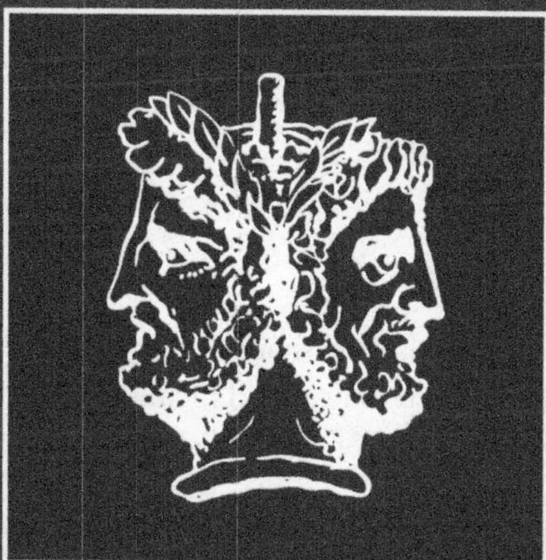

DUTCH N. ALMASBOI

The Janus Deceptions

Published by Wheatmark®
2030 East Speedway Boulevard, Suite 106
Tucson, Arizona 85719 USA
www.wheatmark.com

ISBN: 979-8-88747-327-7 (paperback)
ISBN: 979-8-88747-328-4 (ebook)
LCCN: 2025919398

Bulk ordering discounts are available through Wheatmark, Inc. For more information, email orders@wheatmark.com or call 1-888-934-0888.

This book is a work of fiction.
Though based on and inspired by real people, real places, real events, and in real time, it remains a work of fiction. Any resemblence or inference to real people, living or deceased, is purely intentional and not subject to coincidence.

There are 'writers',
And there are 'those that write'.
This book is dedicated to those dreamers
Who, like me, start out as the latter
And strive to be the former.
And despite our shortcomings, still strive and strive.

But this book is also dedicated to my wife, Janis,
Who upon hearing the proposed title of this work, cried out...
'Oh, no...you can't use my name in the title.
I am not like those kinds of people!'

No, dear, you are not.

"After my marriage, she edited everything I wrote. And what is more, she not only edited my works, she edited me! (of his wife, Livy) —Mark Twain (1835–1910)

Van Wyck Brooks, *The Ordeal of Mark Twain,* 1920

JANUS

Janus is the Roman god of beginnings, endings, and doorways. He is also known as the doorkeeper of the heavens. He has two faces, allowing him to see both inside and outside, and forwards and backwards. He is associated with the transitions between peace and war. His focus is on beginnings, gates, transitions, time, duality, doorways, passages, frames, and endings. He is also known as Lanuspater (Janus Father), Lanus Quadrifrons (Janus Fourfaced), and Lanus Bifrons (two-faced Janus).

It is the latter name that is most appropriate for this mystery novel, as human and material elements of this book evolve around the two-faced hypocrisy that is core to the central theme.

DECEPTIONS

The word is derived as a noun meaning misleading, being dishonest. Examples can include but are not limited to making false statements to misleading claims in which relevant information is omitted, leading the receiver to infer false conclusions. People inclined to deceive are categorized as in the realms of betrayal, deceit, disinformation, duplicity, falsehood, fraud, hypocrisy, lying, mendacity, treachery, trickery and untruths, intentional misleading or beguiling.

To encounter people with Janus-like qualities, and cloak them in the cloudy cover of deception, well…there you have it. The central core with underlying themes of *The Janus Deceptions*.

Enjoy!

But remember:

What sets *The Janus Deceptions* apart from 99% of all other mystery and fiction writings it this: Not only does the reader have to follow along with the mystery *of* the book, he/she also has to figure out the mysteries *within* the book itself.

And that's because…

This novel is 'fiction' at its' best, but it is based on and inspired by some

… real people

… real events

… real places, and

… in real time.

But…what parts?

And that is for you, the reader, to decide! ☺

TABLE OF CONTENTS

Waseca is a small town between Mankato and Rochester in the southern central portion of Minnesota.

C A N A D A
Lake of the Woods
Rainy Lake
Hallock
Roseau
Baudette
Warren
Thief River Falls
Upper Red Lake
Lower Red Lake
Grand Forks
East Grand Forks
Northome
Ely
Eagle Mountain
Grand Marais
NORTH DAKOTA
Bagley
Bemidji
Hibbing
Virginia
Lake Sup
Mahnomen
Grand Rapids
Walker
Two Harbors
Moorhead
Fargo
Detroit Lakes
Duluth
MINNESOTA
MICH
Wadena
Brainerd
Breckenridge
Fergus Falls
Mille Lacs Lake
Alexandria
Little Falls
Pine City
Sauk Centre
Milaca
Morris
St. Cloud
Elk River
Ortonville
SAINT PAUL
Willmar
Litchfield
Brooklyn Park
Plymouth
W I S O N S I N
SOUTH DAKOTA
Montevideo
Hutchinson
Minneapolis
Eau Claire
Granite Falls
Olivia
Bloomington
Lakeville
Redwood Falls
Red Wing
Marshall
New Ulm
Faribault
Waseca
Rochester
Pipestone
St James
Mankato
Owatonna
Windom
Winona
La Crosse
Luverne
Worthington
Blue Earth
Austin
Preston
Fairmont
Albert Lea
Sioux Falls
I O W A

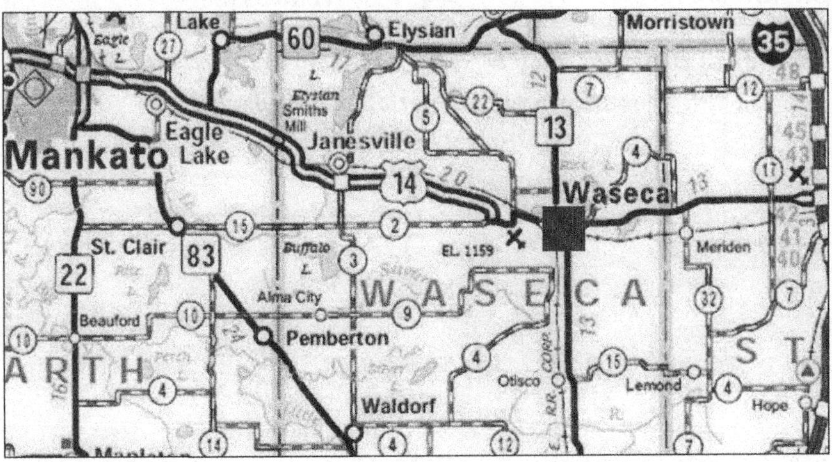
Lake
Eagle L.
60
Elysian
Morristown
35
Elysian L.
Smiths Mill
Eagle Lake
Mankato
Janesville
13
14
Waseca
St. Clair
83
22
EL. 1159
Meriden
Alma City
Pemberton
W A S E C A
Beauford
A R T H
Otisco
Lemond
Waldorf
Hope

PROLOGUE

Writing a mystery novel that is almost entirely set in your hometown can be a daunting task, especially when the writing is taking place over 50 years removed from when you last lived there. But the good, kind, understanding people of Waseca, Minnesota deserve to have another piece of writing with their town as a main part of the focus. It was and is a community worthy of recognition, worthy of attention.

I grew up in Waseca in the 50's and 60's, graduating from Waseca Central High School before going on to the University of Minnesota for my undergraduate and graduate degrees. Waseca was a small, south-central town of about 5,000 people and you could walk anywhere, anytime, and feel safe. Not just because I was a boy, but in general, it was a very good place to grow up. People were friendly, people were working, people were religious, the town was 'clean', and the educational system was one that I was proud to have graduated from, even if some of the teachers were 'old school' and decided discipline was best handled in the janitorial broom closet rather than the confines of the Principal's office! (for the record, I only saw that closet once in my 6 years of junior/senior high…though by rights, I should have seen it more!)

Because of my abilities, I am able to go back and see things exactly as they were, which is critical to the writing of this book. Not only having to recall people, but places, events, times, and actual geographical locations can be daunting…but not for me. I can almost see each leaf that adorns the ground at our 'old 5 acres' plot of bluffed forest west of Otisco, on the Wilton River. That type of memory will be critical as we begin our story in the present, then are forced to go back over 70 years, then work forward to the present again, only to be taken back over 100 years to not only gain access to a critical element in this mystery, but to solve it.

But solving one mystery usually means having to dredge up other things in the past, which lead to other mysteries that need to be reconciled. And sometimes, you just have to face the music and decide now is the time to pay the piper, outcome be damned.

This is what I am faced with in writing this mystery novel… the effect it may have on my family as they discover things not known to them before but having to finally decipher fact from fiction, truth from lies, actualities from fabrication.

But, then again….isn't that what a good mystery is all about?

AUTHOR'S COMMENTS

Samuel Clemons/Mark Twain said it best: 'write what you know'.

It is with that thought front and foremost in my mind that I share with you some preliminary groundwork thoughts before you delve into the world of two faced treachery, murder, and fraud... and come out battered and scathed at the other end, but with a sense of vindication, hope, understanding, and possibly reconciliation.

To start off, this book is based on and includes some real facts, real events, real people, and geographically real places. But there are also elements of fiction woven into the fabric of the story that help give it body, direction, and mystery. It is the combination of those two distinct writing styles...truth and fiction...that are blended into the context of one amazing ride that starts in the present, takes us back to the past, then brings us further along between those two realms, and then dives back even further in time to set the stage for the final battle between 'what happened' and 'what to do about it' decades and a century later.

While I have a documented IQ of 163 with a photographic

memory (the ability to remember and recall information such as pages of text, numbers, or similar or visual images in great detail), I also have an eidetic memory, allowing me the ability to see an object for a few minutes after it is no longer present. This quality was first documented in a Master's Degree research project done in 1963 by the wife of my local dentist, and further documented by entrance examinations afforded me by the Minneapolis office of the FBI during my brief but rewarding undercover assignment with them while a student-athlete at the University of Minnesota. More of that to come in the context of this book!

But I need the reader to know that while this book was a most enjoyable and thrilling journey into my past, you also need to understand that it was also with a great deal of pain and frustration that I was forced to confront parts of my past that I would have preferred to remain buried, with those secrets going with me to my grave. Thinking about past transgressions, let alone bringing them to light, can be either weight lifting or weight bearing, depending on your perspective. And while there is no statute of limitations for the felony crime of murder in the State of Minnesota, giving some people pause to think about pressing charges at this stage of the game may give one time to reflect and re-think whether 'honesty is really the best policy'.

But in the final analysis, yes…honesty is always the best policy; though not necessarily in the timely manner in which many people want it to happen. What was it that Dr. Rev. Martin Luther King once said about '…the truth will set you free…the truth will always win out…'.

Ya, well…with all due respects to your memory and your legacy, the jury may still be out on that one, Rev!

It is very difficult to honor those that have gone before us when deep, dark family secrets are finally revealed…if they are to be revealed at all. Yet, it is with equal understanding that one try to empathize with those individuals present in those times, in those specific, time compressed moments, making those heart-wrenching decisions, without the benefit of hindsight or prognostication. Monday morning quarterbacking was never one of my strong suits, and I have never been an 'I told you so' kind of guy.

But, holy crap…some of this stuff is really important and should have seen the light of day before it came to roost on my laptop computer screen!!! And it came to roost when I was over 70 years old. Now what!?!?!?

So, I take the time to reflect back. I dig, I research, I interview, I travel, I document. I recall with expert detail that which needs to be presented and explained, and I print that which needs to be printed so that the reader will have a complete understanding of what it means:

… to be 'two-faced'…

… to be a 'fraud'…

… to be labeled a 'deceiver'.

—and to finally decide what to do with the remainder of this mortal life.

In spite of, or due to…unintended consequences.

Yes…to be made aware of *The Janus Deceptions.*

INTRODUCTION

December, 2016
Crystal, Minnesota

Yaa!

This has to be one of the best Christmas gift ideas that I have had in years, not only for my wife, Julie, but also for my siblings, my older brother Terry and my older sister Pauline, not to mention the wealth of information that we can leave for our two adult daughters and upcoming grandchildren. For years we have been gathering information from other cousins relative to our family history, its' origins back in the eastern European home country of Prussia and Germany. And now we are on the cusp of actually doing something about it for ourselves.

The impetus for this joy had to originally come from my 'cousin' Desiree Spoettcher of Oregon. She is a DNA expert working with the hospital units in the great northwest not only in the identification of specific DNA strands but also in the wealth of genealogical data that helps identify other family members scattered across the planet.

But I had not met Desiree until my sister and I decided to attend a once-every-4-years family reunion on my mother's side of the family. It has been called the KMM Reunion, which stands for Kanne-Minske-Marzahn…early ancestors that came over in the 1800's and settled mostly in northern Waseca County, a south central county in the state of Minnesota, and home to Waseca, the county seat…where I was born.

While the paternal side of my family can be documented as far back as the early 1700's in Prussia, and emigrated to the United States in the late 1700's and early 1800's, the maternal side is the only side having this 4 year reunion around the 4th of July, held annually in Waseca. My mother, Irma Rathkey, was originally a 'Scarton', and her mother was originally a 'Kanne'…hence, I get included in the fun and games by reason of 'lucky me'!!!

Too bad the paternal 'Rathkey' side of the family doesn't do such formal, social things…guess they had other things on their minds.

Anyway, it was at the 2016 summer reunion that I met cousin Desiree and listened earnestly as she talked about her work in the DNA field and the progress that had been made since its' inception years earlier. I was fascinated sitting in the Waseca United Methodist Church basement listening to Desiree talk, but also smelling the chicken dinner that was being prepared 20 feet from my nose.

Tough for me to concentrate on one and not the other!

But Desiree really hit home when she talked about getting DNA testing done, then having it entered in the national and international data base and see what matches would materialize. My sister, Pauline, seemed eager to check this out, and since we were nearing the 'end' of our particular branch of the 'Rathkey' tree, seemed like a logical and practical thing to do in the upcoming months. I was anxious to get home and share this information with my wife, Julie…she was unable to attend this reunion but would understand my enthusiasm, being a former history teacher herself.

Well, after the reunion was over a day later, weeks turned into months and pretty soon it was getting time to carve up a turkey, give thanks for all we were grateful for, and start holiday shopping.

And I knew exactly what we should do for this Christmas! So it was no surprise when we opened our gifts and found Ancestry 23 testing materials for sister Pauline, Julie, and me…and proceeded to do what needed to be done and sent them off for processing.

Since my sister was retired and did not have a home computer, we set her up on our home computer using our email address as her contact point, but with a separate link so we each could monitor our DNA results and matches in a somewhat private setting. Everything was going great, results would come in and get funneled to a separate folder, and we got to read names and locations from all over the world of distant relatives, usually between 2nd and 4th cousins, but still part of the vital DNA chain.

This went on for several years. Covid hit, but did not seem to affect the rate of information coming in for us to review. It would come in, I would share some of it with Pauline, when I thought of it, and it would get filed away on the computer.

Turns out we did not have the KMM reunion that summer of 2020, but would look forward to the next one in July of 2024 to catch up with relatives and other loved ones we had missed over the years.

This was really great!

Until it wasn't…

Early March, 2024

Crystal, Minnesota

This can't be happening!

All of a sudden my entire world has come crashing down over me, suffocating me as I try to breathe and make sense of what I just saw on the computer screen. This cloud of dread and uncertainty swirls around me like a firenado, making little sense of whatever my senses are telling me at this moment and thrusting me into a deep dive of paralysis.

I just can't make sense of what I am seeing…yet I am seeing it, plain as day, right in front of me. I try to take a deep breath, to regain my composure, but my head is traveling at a million miles an hour with nothing to hold on to that brings me back to my normal sense of reality.

I sit back in my chair, trying to take in all that is around me. My wife's crafting office, located on the first floor of our northwest suburban Minneapolis home in Crystal, has a southern exposure, yet the sunlight that was trying to peek through the clouds minutes ago has vanished into an early spring rain with thunder and lightning waking up the skies.

The overcast nature has a 'downer effect' on my psyche right now, and has amplified not only my visual senses of what I am seeing, but my emotional reaction to that data. I need to step back, take a breath, and try to logically make sense of what I am seeing.

Yes…there has to be a logical explanation as to the phenomena in front of me. I mean, one minute I am looking at promising genealogical email links to my family tree and the next minute I am struck with the distinct possibility that something is dreadfully wrong, something that I have no control over.

Now what do I do?

I

HOW CAN THIS BE?

Crystal, Minnesota
March, 2024

I'm sitting here. A 70 year old retired school superintendent, named Donny Rathkey.

And I am petrified.

I'm seeing it, but I am not believing it.

I am looking at a computer screen that is telling me my sister has hundreds and hundreds of DNA matches over the past several years…people from all over the world and people we don't even know…

And I am not one of them!

Let me explain. When I originally hooked up with Ancestry 23 a few years back I set up three separate accounts so my sister, Pauline, my wife, Julie, and I could put our DNA into the world-wide data base and see evidence of long lost or identified relatives that shared common ancestral heritage with each of us. It was a no brainer that my sister and I would share identical contacts with our Prussian/German heritage while Julie would have a heavier Scandinavian twist with the bulk of her relatives coming from the upper Baltic region.

Well…the old saying goes 'Man makes plans and God laughs' and boy, did he pull a tsunami on me this morning. I just could not believe that while my sister had all of these contacts, I had none.

Nothing. Nada. Zilch.

There had to be something wrong with the set up or with the system, as this was impossible. I went back to the beginning of our ancestral tracking, back several years, and re-read the hundreds and hundreds of identified but unknown to us relatives that shared our common DNA.

But what I was coming up with remained the same: though Pauline and I had separate DNA testing, coupled with separate reporting accounts on my email server, we shared the common server location as she did not have computer access in her apartment. I would simply share with her the information that was sent to me, both her and my contact information, and we would map out where some of the DNA matches lived for purposes of our own historical knowledge.

But not one of those emails came back to me…only to my sister.

And then the cloud of dread began to descend upon the Neanderthal part of my brain and I began to dwell on some dark and horrible thoughts…

Does this mean…?

No…it can't. That would be impossible.

Or…would it? Could it be true?

Is it possible that my older sister, Pauline, is not really my biological older sister?

But, if that is the case, then this expands to the possibility or probability that Bob is not my older brother, and that Terry, called 'Bobber' is not my older brother…

And that Leon and Irma Rathkey are not my biological parents.

Damn…this just got real and a whole lot harder to comprehend. My thoughts are running wild and I am trying my best to contain them through moistened eyes that are fighting the very notions that I have just realized.

But…if this is remotely true…how? When? Where? Who?

My head is now painfully swirling with possible scenarios of which I want none to be true, but… knowing that something has to be true. I am just not sure what that truth is at the present moment…

But I am damn sure gonna find out and put these fears to rest and go on with my life.

But the daunting task of figuring out what has happened and what I need to do to find the truth and bring closure to these horrid feelings has to be done in such a way that does not alarm my sister or my wife or family.

While I am sure they would understand, given all or little that I know at the present, I still don't have any 'proof' of my suppositions or suspicions. To alert anyone to my thoughts at this point in time could be devastating to all involved, and label me more than the 'crazy brother' or 'derelict husband' to those that love me.

Unless that 'someone' was someone who could remain anonymous throughout the process, keep any found information on the down low, and give me advice and direction as to not only what to do, but how to do it and when to do it in order to achieve accurate and reliable results.

Yes, there has to be a person with not only the technical skills necessary for guiding me but also a person that has a stake in the outcome, someone that has experience in this type of investigation and is empathetic to my situation. Someone who can identify with the pain I am going through and at least show me the way ahead, no matter what the outcome, and be with me on the 'other side' of the results.

There has to be a person…there has to be a person…someone…

Yes…yes…there is.

And she lives in Oregon!

2

PANIC AND DIRECTION

Crystal, Minnesota
Late March, 2024

Having met my 'cousin' Desiree Spoettcher a few years back, and being in touch a few times over the internet since then, Desiree was most cordial and welcoming when I called her on the phone later on that month. I needed some time to fully grasp not only what I was seeing in front of me on that damn computer screen but also process the probability and possibility of the resolution that I was hoping to achieve.

I was in full panic mode when this journey started and have since calmed down, something that Desiree was most ably suited for when talking with me over the phone. She understood the situation and my concerns, and did her best to sway me to her line of thinking about 'what we know and what we don't know' so that my panic mode did not go into hyperdrive when it needed to be my old self: cool, calm, collected.

I explained the entire situation to Desiree over a 2 hour phone call, and while we got interrupted a few times with little ones on her end of the line back home, we stayed together for the duration of the conversation. What it boiled down to was this:

If my fears were to be alleviated, we needed evidence that could be objectively tested and give us reasonably good grounds to proceed with further testing, analysis, and prognosis.

Sounds like a damn doctoral thesis is taking shape…something that both Desiree and I have in common! But I am in her hands on this one and will follow her guidance every step of the way.

For the record, my father, Leon, always had a saying, amongst other sayings: "when you have the opportunity to set the record straight, you set the record straight'. Well, Dad…it looks like I am in this one up to my eyeballs and need to either set the record straight or lock step in behind it and let it lead me down a new path.

Desiree laid out a plan, explaining to me the various steps that we needed to take along the way, from (1) identifying DNA materials that could be tested to (2) the collection of said materials and finally to (3) the actual testing and (4) reading or interpretation of the results. In reality, there is no interpretation necessary when it comes to DNA…DNA does not lie. It just 'is' and you have to accept the results. There is no room for error.

Desiree suggested that since my sister, Pauline, is my closest living blood relative (older brother Terry lives in Albuquerque, New Mexico and oldest brother, Bob, has since passed) and we don't want to get our daughters involved at this early in the juncture, she would be my target for DNA location and extraction… my only decision was whether or not to tell her ahead of time and let her in on what my secreted suspicions were, or not.

I chose the latter.

First of all, I love my sister dearly and would not intentionally want to hurt her in any way, shape, form, or manner…unless it was unavoidable. And in this case, at this point in time, any amount of pain or consternation she would suffer could and would have to be avoidable.

So I chose to do this on the down low, as soon as feasible,

and to follow Desiree's plans for collection, labeling, sterilization, and security for transportation all while not letting anyone else in the family in on the process. The material collected has to include bodily fluids (blood, mucous, spit, tears, etc.) or body attachments (hair strands with the root still attached to the stem of the follicle).

Well, that seemed easy enough to do. I knew what to get, where to get it from, how to secure it in airtight baggies or swab collection containers, and how to get it Fed Ex'd to Desiree overnight so that she could get busy with testing and analysis on her end up in her hospital lab in Oregon.

Oh, this is just gonna be another walk in the park, isn't it, Donny?

And, I'm gonna pull this off without my wife, Julie, knowing anything about it? How about my sister, Pauline, since it's gonna take place in her apartment? And what about my two adult daughters, Tristan and Cynthia…they are equally gifted and intelligent and to be honest, the better part of me. Julie and I really did good on those two!!! How do I keep a straight face and not give away any of my fears while trying to be the 'same old Dad' as time goes by? Don't ask me…I am winging this one right and left and am ready to jump from the pan into the fire and hope I don't get burned before I need to get burned.

Guess it's time for Sherlock Rathkey to make an appearance.

3

SHERLOCK RATHKEY

St. Paul, Minnesota
Early April, 2024

My older sister, Pauline, is a retired employee of the University of Minnesota. She was born a few years after Dad got back from military service during WW II, in fact, sharing the same birthday as him...September 1. But her birth in 1947 and mine in 1953 may be only 6 years difference, but we are much closer than those years indicate.

You see, my father was born in 1909 and my mother in 1915. They married in 1935 and started a family a couple of years later, with older brother Bob being born in 1937 and older brother Terry joining the herd in 1941. Pauline and I rounded out the family and I was really closer to her in many ways than my older siblings, especially considering the significant age difference. In many ways, my parents ages were similar to the age of many classmates grandparents' as I was growing up...something I just adjusted to.

But while having a superior intelligence quotient, Pauline had several physical limitations and conditions that led to an early retirement from the U to her apartment in the nearby suburb of St. Anthony Park in St. Paul, just off the fair grounds and the St. Paul campus of the U of M. It is a 'safe' location and quite accessible to all that she needs to be in touch with: friends, medical attention, transportation services, shopping, etc. And with me coming over at least once a month to help out with shopping or other errands, we see each other on a fairly regular basis.

On a fairly regular basis…that's it! That's the cover I need to collect the evidence!

I can combine a 'shopping' trip for her with having to use her restroom for a few minutes (now that was done on a regular basis!) and she would never be the wiser. But I need to be efficient as well as effective. I need to get in quietly, act quickly and without noise or suspicions, and leave with the materials without looking like I just robbed a Target outlet store with pockets full of goodies!

So I thought ahead and decided to combine my heist with her mid-April shopping trips to Walmart, Office Depot, Target, Batteries Plus, and Cub Foods. This was the routine I followed every couple of months for Pauline, getting both dental and hygienic items at one place, then getting home office supplies at another, while finishing up with kitchen supplies and major food pickups my last stop before going to her apartment. Every once in a while one of her watches would need battery replacement, so I would make that stop as well.

But once I got back to her apartment, I would usually help her unload the perishable items first so they could get put in the freezer or refrigerator, then leave the 'other' items in bags for her to unload at her leisure as the day went on. It was not unusual for me to need to use the restroom before we went over the billing for each location, going line item by line item so she knew where prices had changed or where I made a decision to maximize her purchasing power by getting a 'better' deal for her buck…something she trusted me to do on my own, but still…I want her to know and be informed. Living on a fixed income budget of social security and pension makes one count not only the nickels and quarters but also the pennies these days. I didn't want her wasting her monies where she didn't need to.

And there you have it…I feel like a cheat, a liar, and a thief… all in one.

I feel like a cheat for not telling Pauline about what was going on and what I needed to do, but I left, knowing that my cause had an ulterior motive and that since we did not know factually where things were, the less she knew the better, at least at this point in time. It still didn't make me feel any better, but I felt it was what I had to do.

I also felt like a liar in not telling Pauline about my contact with Desiree Spoettcher, a person she would have remembered from our last joint trip to Waseca for the KMM family reunion back in 2016. But, again…I believed it best at this point in time to remain silent.

But the real pain I felt was that I was not only feeling but acting like a thief in the securing of the DNA items that Desiree said were essential for testing purposes. I was literally taking 'things' of Pauline's that, though in the waste basket, were in her waste basket and still in her possession, not on the street in a container waiting for Waste Management to come along and pick up with the rest of the trash.

(Those same feelings…liar, cheat, and thief, will come up again down the road…several times. Not good feelings to have and not ones I like to share, but I must, since there are many truths that must be exposed in order for final resolutions to be reached).

Time to put plans into action. Shopping day is here and I need to get a move on.

Well, mid April is here, I am in Pauline's apartment on Brewster Avenue and have just put things away and need to use the restroom. While Pauline is keeping to herself putting away some paper products (and making some noise in the process, which will help cover any unnecessary noises I may make) I immediately take out two baggies and pull some hair samples with full follicle endings from Pauline's hairbrush located on the back of her toilet. I want to take two samples since Pauline often uses baby powder in smooth her dry skin, and I don't want our sample to be contaminated with said powder if I can at all help it. So, double samples it is.

After putting those two samples in my pants pockets I switch my attention to her wastebasket where I strike the DNA mother load. Pauline often gets nosebleeds due to the dry air in her apartment, and there are several Kleenex tissues with significant and recent blood samples that I place into zip lock baggies and put into the front pouch of my Cabela's hoody.

Along with that are several 'clean' Kleenex tissues with mucous droppings that can also be used for DNA analysis, so they go into two separate baggies and find their way into the back pockets of my pants. This entire process has taken about 2 minutes, so I immediately flush the toilet, as if I had used it, then turn on the sink faucet to wash my hands, which I did do after sample collections. A quick wipe on the towel and I am out of there, saying goodbye to my sister, and hoping she does not suspect any bulges in my pockets as I exit the door and get in my truck.

Luckily for me, Pauline's vision is blocked by where I parked outside, so she does not see me take the two samples from my rear pockets and the two samples from my front pockets and combine them with the two samples from my hoody pouch into a cooler bag on my passenger front seat. Desiree had instructed me to try and keep the samples as cool as possible…not frozen, but cool…to help preserve the 'integrity' of the samples before the actual testing was to begin.

And I intended to follow her instructions to the letter of the law. This was not the time to screw up, Donny, though worst case scenario means the samples were wasted and another set would have to be collected at some point in time, as soon as possible, if necessary. Let's hope I did it right the first time and the second effort would not be necessary.

With hair samples, blood samples, and bodily fluids samples in my possession, I headed back to Crystal to get things ready to send to Desiree...unaware that my sister had followed me down to the front door of her apartment complex (to wave goodbye to me) and was wondering what was taking me so long getting into my truck to drive home?

If she only knew...'Sherlock' Rathkey had done his duty.

But what would be the result...and the cost...down the road once this information became known?

4

GOD I HOPE THIS WORKS

Crystal, Minnesota
One day later, April, 2024

Driving the 30 minutes home back to our northwest suburban home in Crystal, I kept thinking about the 'ruse' I had just pulled over my sisters' eyes and how I would tell her the truth, once the truth finally became known. But while my eyes were misting up again at the prospect of not liking what I was about to do, I had to focus on doing that which I felt was right and just under the existing conditions and circumstances.

There are unknowns out there, and to put my head in the sand and pull an ostrich move, or to throw the Harry Potter 'veil of invisibility' over the entire situation did not bode well with my personality nor my demeanor.

My entire life in education and educational administration centered around my 'core' personality of being a 'change agent'. I was not hired or brought in to 'baby sit' the status quo. I was brought in to change things and make a difference based on what I observed, research, and the direction I believed would lead us to a better position down the road.

Well, this was certainly within my wheel house…a possible

'change' in the status quo that would shake not only my foundation but that of our entire family. But while I don't want to get the cart before the horse, we have to just follow 'presumed innocent until proven guilty' even in this scenario. We have no evidence at this point in time, only theory with some potential samples to be tested and analyzed.

So, let's get on with the direction the theory points us to go.

Damn the torpedoes…full speed ahead!

I realized on the way home I needed to contact Desiree right away as to handling instructions so I drive around the block and park a few hundred yards away so I can use my cell phone rather than go home and use the landline, unaware of where Julie may be and what she may overhear.

I get ahold of Desiree, tell her what I have done, and am awaiting further instructions so these samples can get to her with all due haste. We go over the shipping requirements, as the samples need to be separated in the shipping container (which I have already done with separate zip lock baggies and blood collecting vials) and the need for the container to be as cool as possible during shipment.

In addition to Pauline's samples, I have already taken 2 samples of my own blood, put them in blood collecting vials, and sealed them. I also took 2 samples of my own hair and secured them in a separate ziplock baggie, and since I also have a cold at the time, was easily able to collect several Kleenex with mucous and bodily fluids for additional testing analysis. I figure with what I have of Pauline's, and what I have of mine for comparison, the testing lab should be able to conduct several runs of the DNA for analysis and be able to definitively tell us one way or another if we are blood brother and sister…or something else.

Instructions received, I know what to do, and now I am really nervous. Desiree can sense my concerns so we talk for awhile as she talks me 'down' to the realities of what I have done, but not the outcomes, as of yet. Those are down the road, and we will deal with them when the time comes.

I feel better, let her know I will tend to things within the hour, and proceed home to see my wife and try to be as normal as possible after a very abnormal day. For some reason, this starts me laughing, as this reminds me of hunchback Marty Feldman in the Gene Wilder movie 'Young Frankenstein', when Feldman is describing the brain sample of 'A.B. Normal' that just got transplanted into the brain of the monster.

Now all I need is the open fireside farting scene from 'Blazing Saddles' to put me over the edge!

I get back home and find Julie out in the backyard moving around some small plants to other locations in the garden. Seemed a bit early to me, but hey…early spring in Minnesota and you do what you can and want to do when the weather allows you to be outside. And Julie loves the sunlight and warm temperatures, and while still a true Minnesotan at heart, some fresh air is good for the soul.

I let her know I am done with Pauline's errands, but have something of hers that I need to mail via Fed Ed, so if she does not mind, I will get after that and be home in plenty of time to grill outside for supper. I already have 2 ribeye steaks thawing in the refrigerator for such an occasion, plus this will buy me the time/excuse I need to get to Maple Grove and get this package in the proper container and shipped so Desiree will get it overnight.

Maple Grove, a very affluent northwest suburb of Minnespolis, is only 15 minutes away, and the Fed Ex place is really quiet this early in the afternoon, so things go quickly for me.

And, true to expectations, I leave Fed Ex with about $78 less in my checking account due to the specialized handling and packaging requirements necessary for this DNA package to reach Oregon overnight, but, what the heck. I know it will get there with the most care that can be given a 'special' package marked 'fragile'.

Should have included the words 'Caution: venomous reptile inside' and see it that provided any better handling!

So, for now…all is out of my hands.

I confronted the situation.

I consulted expert direction.

I gathered specific evidence.

I transferred evidence to the expert in charge.

I sit back and await the outcome.

God, I can only hope that this works! Whatever the outcome, it will be the right outcome.

But which side of 'right' will I be on?

5

EARLY REFLECTIONS

Waseca, Minnesota
1953-1957

As I sit in my great room recliner in our Crystal home, with Julie off running errands, I find myself anxiously awaiting word from Desiree relative to the DNA testing that she and her lab are about to undertake.

But I also find myself drifting back to another time in my life… way back…to the earliest memories that I have of 'life' and those around me, wondering…'was there some clues that I missed, or can pick up along the way, to help me clear up this situation' or am I just adding more worry and misery and speculation to a situation that I had and have no control over?

As I reflect back to 'early' Waseca, and my most vivid recollections of memories, I find that, despite my advanced intellectual abilities and gifts of recall, I am at a near loss for trying to remember anything from those very early years. Granted, I am talking about memories from birth to about age 4, but still…what can I recall that may shed some light, no matter how insignificant it may seem, to my predicament?

I can recall an old house a block north and across the main

street of the one that I grew up in as a young boy. This two story house was built on a stone foundation with a detached single car garage. There were neighbors on both north and south sides of this house and homes up and down this part of the main drag, which was Highway 13 going north out of town.

I can remember one memory of being in a baby buggy that was an old pink/pale pink kind of color with 4 big wheels and a large handle in the back for pushing. It had a flat bottom, not one that could recline for the comfort of the occupant; hey, this was the early 1950's...comfort was not on the main menu of options for baby strollers!

I remember my older brother pushing me in that stroller down the front steps at this house and then pushing me toward the sidewalk that ran north and south parallel to the highway, and we went for a walk to the south around this huge block. It must have been the equivalent of two city blocks today, as it was long and about 100 yards deep east to west. It was a nice ride...but that is all I got.

I remember another memory of sitting on the toilet, being told I had to 'do my business' before I could go out and play with the other kids in the neighborhood. But who in their right mind wants to play with a 3-4 year old, and will wait for me to take a crap before we start a game of whatever?

But what I also remember from that bathroom experience was three distinct things:

1. When I was done pooping, I had to call my mother in to wipe my bottom as evidently this was not something I could do on my own at the time. But as later memories would occur and come back to me, this same situation repeated itself many and many and many times over in our 'new' home to the point where I can still remember this same routine later on in my elementary school life even as a 4th grader in Ms. Fell's class at Hartley elementary school.

That thought alone is enough to make me want to stop writing this book right now. But I must continue, I must recall and face the consequences of my memory, no matter how twisted they were at the time and how ugly they now seem decades later.

2. Also, while sitting on that toilet seat I recalled seeing a mouse run along the floor to my right, then scurry around the corner and it was gone. I never told anyone about what I saw…I didn't have to. For it was the next memory that caused me to vomit all over the place and not want to recall the memory at all.
3. My mother and sister Pauline were baking cookies in the kitchen while I was doing bathroom duties, and it was the smell of those cookies that I identified with that mouse, and to this day I cannot smell or eat a certain kind of sugar cookie because the 'smell' of that mouse coupled with the smell of the cookies made for a very unappetizing feeling in my stomach.

And to this day my wife, Julie, does not make those cookies at all…but she does it for another reason and not the one that I identified above. There is no way I am going to tell her that her cookies remind me of mice and pooping and bad elementary dreams. Well, at least not until this book comes out! Sorry, honey…cat is out of the bag!

The last memory I have of my earliest childhood from the north end of town was a sad memory for me, but to this day, is as crystal clear as if it happened yesterday.

My grandfather Rathkey was born around 1869 and lived his whole life in Waseca. He was 87 years old when he died, the same age as my father when he passed; believe me, I already have that year circled on my calendar and hope to God I can get to it and through it as quickly as possible…that is my life expectancy goal!

Anyway, while you will hear of Grandpa Hans in upcoming

chapters, the memory that stands out for me here is that my only… repeat…my ONLY memory of him is him lying in his casket at the Methodist Church in Waseca, the day of his funeral.

I can see him as clearly as there is sunlight outside: his stoic face, his German nose and features, his smaller than prime physical body size which seemed to shrink as he aged. But most of all, I remember a feature I myself have to this very day:

I remember his mustache.

You see, my grandfather did not wear facial hair like some others would with sideburns and a full beard, but he had a great mustache that would rival that of any aged caterpillar in the neighborhood!

Ah…but he wore it for a reason…the same as me! And now is the time for that reason to be revealed.

My grandfather, like me, had a skin condition that affected the area just above his upper lip and under his nose, and ran the length of this area. While he and I are able to shave other parts of our face without any noticeable trauma, trying to shave this area caused significant irritation resulting in tender skin, reddening of the skin area, and sometimes blisters would arise.

So…the logical solution to the problem was not to shave in that area.

He didn't, and neither have I since the first day of my freshman year at the University of Minnesota back in 1971. Well, there was this 2 week period back in 1973 when my girlfriend was pissed at me and I shaved it off just for spite. But it was then I realized that while I don't consider myself a handsome man in many senses of the word, I am not butt ugly, either. But not having a mustache was a really big mistake and it would never happen again, and hasn't in the last 50+ years.

But…back to the memories.

That very vivid memory of my grandfather in his casket has stayed with me ever since that day late in 1956. My grandmother

Izzy Rathkey would pass away less than 90 days later, so my father lost both his parents in the span of 3 months. True to my grandfathers wishes, my parents tore down that multi-story home just a block south of our north Waseca home in spring of 1957, used the salvaged timber and built a 'new' Rathkey family home on the site of where my father grew up and lived as a young boy. The home was designed by my mother (what a marvelous architect) and built by the best local carpenter money could buy…though money was not the key variable in building our new home.

I remember that… as we would walk south from our home on the west side of the street and watch the progress being made in the construction. I was 3 and ½ at that time, and would be 4 years old when we moved in later that same fall.

That memory is clear as a bell, as if I took that walk yesterday. But while a few memories still exist, I am not seeing any early clues that 'something' was off or may have been 'wrong', something that indicated that I did not belong here…it's still too early to put my finger on anything here from the past.

But the day is coming when that is going to change.

And that day is coming soon.

But as I sit in my present day recliner, thinking and looking back, those are the only major memories that I have from those very early years. I think my memory 'gifts' and talents are not going to fully develop until I get alittle bit older. But when they kick in, and I mean kick in…there is gonna be some thunder and lightening that comes reigning down from the heavens and stirs up some very evil and ugly thoughts about not only what I have done or are going to do…but the coverup that has stayed hidden for all these years.

They say that confession is a good cleanser of the soul.

Sorry….I am not Catholic.

And what I am going to remember and bring to the surface may just have me seeing the inside of a prison for the rest of my life.

6

SILENCE IS NOT GOLDEN

Crystal, Minnesota
June, 2024

Sitting here waiting for a call from Desiree is like waiting to pass a kidney stone. You know it's gonna hurt and there is not a damn thing you can do to prevent it. You just have to brace yourself, grin and bear it, and hope that you can still screw once your penis gets back to its' normal shape and condition.

Damn…my grandkids are gonna read this book some day, aren't they? Oh, well…give me some latitude. I am a 70 year old man with a pissed off attitude and am awaiting news…probably bad news…but news nonetheless that could severely have my life taking a huge left turn at exactly the moment I don't need it to.

Reflecting back on those very early years also brought a small level of comfort as I relived some memories that had been dormant for a very long time. But the reality of that dormancy only magnified the question…

Will those be memories of 'my family' when this is all said and done, or will they just be memories of 'another' family that happened to be one I was inserted into?

I know, I know…quit being such a pessimist and look on the bright side of things.

Who in their right mind thinks there is a 'right' side to this situation, especially since we are still in the dark?

Julie has run to Target to get a few things. I am reading another James Patterson novel, and then the phone rings.

I look at the display, recognize the number and the state, and know who is calling.

Desiree!

I quickly pick up the receiver and in a higher pitched voice that I have not heard since junior high squeak out a 'hi' to my cousin.

And then I wilt in my recliner, awaiting the verdict.

Less than 10 minutes later I hang up the phone, perplexed yet very calmly at peace with myself. Desiree has shared that the results just came in, but it is her 'professional' policy and position to only share those results with the person involved 'in-person', 'face to face' at my earliest convenience.

I realize that reality has now come home to roost and I must do two things, and not necessarily in any order. I share my thoughts with Desiree, to which she concurs.

I cannot in all good conscience try to 'hide' a plane ticket to Oregon from my wife at this point in time, but I also cannot tell her or my family where things 'are' without putting them through a period of anguish awaiting the same results that I am waiting for.

Nobody needs the additional stress at this point in time, and if I am the only one to bear that burden of the unknown, at least for another month or so, then so be it.

Desiree and I agree to speak in person at the earliest opportunity come July, 2024…one month down the road…at the next installment of the KMM family reunion. She will have all available DNA testing information for me to review, and she will also have a professional assistant that she often travels with there for support since I will be coming alone. She reminds me that this is not a 'sign' of things to come; she always travels with support personnel so that her clients have another person to talk with should the need arise. I concur…good idea.

Not a sign, my ass! This has the smell of roquefort and texture of liver…not a good combination. But I take Desiree at her word and prepare to go about the next month doing things I would normally do, and show, on the 'outside', while on the inside my guts are just churning like a fast moving Beer Barrel Polka what won't slow down.

There have been many times in the past where one must swallow their own pride and do not just the 'right thing' but 'what is right'…those things are not mutually identical. And I now find myself in a position where I just have to be 'cool, calm, collected' Donny and go about life as if nothing has changed.

And, to a degree…nothing has changed. We are simply awaiting news to see if something has changed.

And, if something has changed, has it only changed things in the past, or also the present and God forbid…the future?

Guess we just have to wait to find that out. I can't predict what is going to be told me nor how I will react to that news. I can only prepare (i.e. 'steel' myself) to the possibility that I will not like the upcoming news but at the same time can't be overwhelmed by it.

Remaining silent is my only prudent option at this juncture, with both my wife and my family.

But, oh….Pauline. This news could destroy her in short order, and since she wears her emotions on her sleeve, this is something that could really send her over the edge into a place that none of us want to go.

So…what those myriads of thoughts running around my head like a tribe of neutered banchees, I ready myself for what seems to me to be an impossible month of silence in which the status quo is your friend and things will be all right.

Easy for you to say…you're just reading this.

I have to endure it…

7

YOUNG REFLECTIONS

Waseca, Minnesota
1957-1961

Finding myself in a holding pattern while awaiting my personal visit with Desiree Spoettcher is like waiting for a pitched curve ball and wondering which of several options you have and will take: (1) do you wait for it to come closer, then bail out of the hitter's box; (2) do you wait for it to come closer, only to have it come too close and hit you; (3) do you wait for it to come closer, swing and miss because you didn't wait long enough; or (4) do you wait for it to come closer, wait for the break, and knock the hell out of it for a homerun?

I used to be a pretty good baseball player back in my day. My fielding prowess at 1st base got me the nickname 'Hoover' while playing baseball, and my catching abilities behind the plate earned me the nickname 'Block' because nothing got by me, nothing got through me, and nothing got around me.

But sitting here waiting for the inevitable or what may seem to be inevitable is just not my cup of tea…I never was just a 'sitter' waiting for things to happen.

I learned over the years that there are three types of people: (1)

those that sit back and wait for things to happen; (2) those that sit back and as things go by, wondered 'what happened'?; and (3) those that make things happen. Thank God I have the personality for the latter, for the former two options just don't cut it for me.

But as I sit here contemplating what may be in my immediate future, I find myself drifting back to my remembered past, only this time I have gone from being a 3-4 year old little squirt to a 4-8 year old terror!

I now look back at those years after we moved from our 'old' house in the north end of town to a block south, in our 'new' house, built on the site of my father's childhood home and where my paternal grandparents lived all their lives.

But, boy…what a change to the neighborhood! While the neighborhood has not seen new construction in probably 50 years, the house my mother designed and had built would have made Frank Lloyd Wright stand up and take notice.

Gone was the two story, wooden framed 'old' square house and in its' place is a one story, many windowed wooden and stone piece of art. This home is so far advanced and modern that it actually looks out of place for the neighborhood, not only in its' forward thinking design but also the use of property space and beauty.

Gone are the drab colors of the olden neighborhood style and in comes a white house with pink trim on the outside, with massive picture windows maximizing its' southern exposure. But one also has to remember that living in a house with so much glass means that not only can you look out and enjoy the scenery of the neighborhood, so can the neighborhood look in and see what is going on in the Rathkey home!

That lesson will come back to haunt me many times growing up!

But, enough of the house analysis. Moving into this new house at 4 years of age just gave me some new places to play, things to get into, and people to meet. New neighbors, soon to be new school chums, and lots of places to get into things as only a little boy can do.

But as memory serves me, this little boy, over the next 4 years, is starting to get into things that will stretch the limits of not only his experiences but also the patience and temperament of not only his mother and father, but that of his older siblings

I was 4 years old in the late fall of 1957 when we moved to our new home on North State Street, just a block south of our original home further north. That meant we were only 6 blocks from the heart of downtown Waseca…the junction of Highway 14 going east and west and Highway 13 going north and south. It was Janesville and Mankato to the west; Otisco, New Richland and eventually Albert Lea to the south; Owatonna and Rochester further to the east; and Waterville and eventually the Twin Cities to the north.

What a great location and place to live!

And what a great time to remember clues and inklings that this was a place that I was not supposed to be in.

Being sent to Kindergarten at the Congregational Church in the fall of 1958 as a still-4 year old was challenging, even with my neighbor Mrs. Hanson across the street being my teacher. She was great, as was her husband 'Sven' and her kids Barry, a classmate of my older brother, Terry, and daughter Mary, or 'Fairy' as she was known. She was also a baby sitter of mine…

But only for a few times.

I seem to remember some 'things' that happened between us that made her not want to come back and sit with me. Perhaps it was my acting out, perhaps my rambunctious nature, or perhaps my naughtiness at not following directions.

I never was very good at that 'two ears and one mouth' kind of philosophy, even at an early age. And I remember her telling my mother that I was 'more than a handful' to be able to control and that I acted out 'viciously' when confronted with having to do things that I didn't want to do.

Over the next couple of years this behavior would repeat and become more noticeable when other babysitters would show up once, and not again. I remember those days, and those evil girls that tried to get me to do things that I did not want to do.

If you don't want me to act this way, stop telling me to do things I don't want to do.

Memories of standing behind the garage with my father looking at the corn stalks that were growing in the garden was a pleasing memory…until I went over and knocked several of the stalks down, to the ire of my father. That spanking was probably deserved, but in the garden? With Mrs. Finks, Mrs. Rowell, Mrs. Fagen, and old lady Thompson able to hear my wailing?

Well, that seemed very unfair to me. Plus…the corn was ready to be picked. So what was the big deal? But I do remember that it was my father who always did the spanking, while my mother stood by and watched or turned her head at my cries. The old 'wait until your father gets home' routine soon became very routine, and while I did not enjoy the hand spankings, as soon as it went to the yardstick, well, that added a whole new element to my psychological makeup...

…how much could I take and not react to? No cries, no wails, just enduring pain.

Was this the earliest that I can remember of signs and clues that something was 'wrong' with me? Then, and years later, I would always hear stories of my older siblings and their 'perfect' accomplishments, be it in the arena of school, church, scouts, community service, personal accomplishments, musical abilities…

I was always being told of this, as if this was the 'gold' standard by which I would be measured. But what if I was not like them, in all of those different arenas?

What if I was different?

But while still very young, I was starting to notice a direct correlation between my behaviors (or misbehaviors, as they may be) and how I was treated. Going from Kindergarten, which was right across the street from the high school where an older brother and sister were attending school,. to 1st grade the next fall in that same building…that, was a real eye opening experience.

I now had a larger area to get into things, a larger audience from which to observe other behaviors of older students, and more opportunity on the walk to school or to home in which to vary my routes to learn new, exciting places to get into trouble!

Again, the more I got into trouble exploring things as a little boy, the more my butt hurt and it seemed, the worse the clothes I had to wear when outside either playing with others or going to school with my peers. Suddenly I was aware of others not wanting to play as much with me, and other school students not wanting to sit near me either in the classroom or at lunch or on the playground.

So, I learned to be my own best friend. Or enemy. Or enabler, whatever the circumstances called for. I still acted out, I still misbehaved, and I still got into trouble. I think the corner of our great room had my name permanently etched on the wall I spent so much time there, facing it.

Spankings continued, but now as a 7-8 year old going to a new elementary school, Hartley Elementary, located about 3 long blocks east of our home just alongside the baseball and football fields (on an old garbage dump that was filled in) I found myself in a new part of town where I could spend time learning new things, with new people along the way to and from school, and try to test the patience of my new, almost all female, teaching staff!

My new, almost all, single female teaching staff!

But with a principal, Mr. Severson, that also used his belt as punishment for deeds warranting such admonishment. While we were on a first name basis so much I thought my desk in his outer office was a place I could now get my mail, he never once used his belt on me. Took it off, once. Held it in his hand, once, but never used it on me.

And now I was beginning to understand 'why'.

From an early age I started to see that the 'Rathkey' name carried some significant weight...actually, a great deal of weight…in this town. While people were always, and I mean always friendly to my mother and father, I also gleaned that they were people not of physical means but of 'stature' and 'kindness' to everyone they met. I did not come from a wealthy family in terms of monetary resources, but when you have two older brothers in college, a sister getting ready to go there, and you bringing up the rear with people hoping you would amount to something, well…you get the picture.

But the visible kindness and graciousness that others saw was just that…others saw it.

I didn't.

All during my early years I can't recall (and I have perfect recall) my mother saying 'I love you' or 'I'm sorry' once to me.

Not once.

My father, when confronted with a contradiction where I was 'right' in a particular situation when he thought I was wrong, was just a shrug of his shoulders, a smile, and a comment like 'well, let that be a lesson to you'.

Now, don't get me entirely wrong. My father was a very kind man and to my dying day I will remember those kindnesses. But I also remember the tough times, the hard times, the times that I made not only mistakes but choices that made his life more difficult than it needed to be. But my father was not an 'I told you so' man, and neither did I become one.

I guess those days of 'tough love' and 'old school lessons' were the way things were done back then, and as time went on, as people grew up, you either had a choice to stick to those same old methods with your own children or you could stand up with courage, break with the past, and forge ahead with 'new' ways to discipline and teach and bring up your children .

But I did learn the difference between 'discipline' and 'punishment'. And with me, it was always the harder lesson involving punishment. You start to grow a set, even at a young age, and my early days from Kindergarten through Grade 1-2 were coming to a close. Soon it would be time to play with the bigger boys and girls, and there was a whole new set of rules and regulations, both written and social, that I would have to learn if I was to survive the viciousness of young life.

But again I am drawn back to early signs, early clues that something was wrong, was out of place, that I did not belong in this setting. And all I can come up with is some verbal, some non-verbal, and some physical actions that resulted from my misbehaviors at the time.

Other clues would soon be appearing, but that would start more in my late elementary and early junior high years. For now, things are still somewhat cloudy but vivid memories are beginning to appear, and there is a specific reason for that formation.

My parents, at least once a month, would take us (mom, dad, Pauline, myself) and whatever older brothers happened to be home, and go downstairs into what we called our furnished basement: fireplace, record player, cabinetry area, radio, piano, dining room table, sofa, church bench in front of a blackboard, cool storage/wood storage/storm cellar and an under the steps storage area that housed God knows what! My grandfather Hans' pipe stand sat on the floor next to the sofa, and this was a place where we could spend some quality relaxing time, Christmas tree when the season called for it…it was great!

But in that storage area were two of my favorite items: a portable screen projector and an 8 mm film projector that played home films shot by my parents. Just the smell of the old screen as you set it up put you in the mood for watching old home movies, and the smell of the projector as it ran, with the noise it made, let you know you were alive!

Like I said, at least once a month we would gather downstairs for a few hours and look at these movies, possibly having some goodies that mom made for such a time, as we were all relaxed with no concerns about dropping crumbs on the concrete floor or the two rugs from our 'old' home that held the sofa and dining room table.

But as I watched the movies, this was where I learned my family history, and it went back decades. Old fishing trips up north, family graduations and outings, picnics and family get togethers, church activities…you name it, it was on those movies.

But what I was noticing was not only 'who' was on the movies, but who was 'not' on the movies, especially as time went on. Lots of early movies with my older brothers and sister and family members, but after 1953…the year of my birth…not so much of 'Donny' in those pictures.

Oh, I would show up now and then, here and there, but not the 'doting' child that my older siblings were fawned over in their youth. And those visuals began to weigh on my mind, subconsciously, to the point where going down to see these old family movies was becoming less and less inviting for me.

It was all, or almost all, about others…not Donny.

It was all, or almost all, about other people and the fun they were having…not Donny.

While there were obligatory times that I had to appear on the camera, there were smiles all around. But as I look back at those early pictures, I was wondering how much of that smiling was for the camera or out of relief, rather than actual joy.

I was starting to see correlations between others and me…

I was starting to see correlations between past times and present times and how it affected me…

I was starting to see the diminished visuals surrounding me as time went on…

I was starting to see my parents age in front of my eyes, and the effect it was having on me…

I was starting to see…and I didn't like what I was seeing.

The signs were there. The clues were there.

And now I was seeing them right in front of me.

As a kid, I was beginning to realize that I was different than those other people, those other brothers and sister, those other relatives…

I was beginning to feel like an outsider, looking in, rather than an insider looking out.

And, yes, I began acting out more and more and being more of a terror than I should have been. I saw my mother struggling with these misbehaviors and the reaction she would have to my acting out and mischievous doings.

But I didn't care.

I kept it up. And up. And up. And the 'dark' side of Donny's personality was starting to bloom, and while he would try to keep it hidden most of the time, it would rear its' head like a threatened rattler and strike when one was least expecting it.

Until one day, the dam burst and all Hell was going to come crashing down.

My mother's vidaliam prescription was running low. She was getting a suitcase from the hall storage closet. I saw my father in his Deputy Sheriff's uniform, and he was not smiling.

A new threat was in town: The Sheriff's Boys Ranch….and it was reserving a spot for me!

Oh, damn…and I am only in 2nd grade!

8

WHISKEY TANGO FOXTROT

Waseca, Minnesota
July 13, 2024

Well, this damn waiting period is almost over. It is a cloudy day here in the Twin Cities, and I am leaving our Crystal home to head south to Waseca for the every-4th-year KMM family reunion. This all happens on account of my mother's ancestors, but it is still a good time to catch up especially with those older relatives that I remember from my youth and like all of us, are 'on the clock' for the final countdown.

As I drive south at 6am in the morning on Interstate 35W I find myself drifting to thoughts of 'what if' or 'what do I do now' rather than just listening to 106.1 Bob FM, my favorite country radio station out of Albertville.

Oh, crap…early Saturday morning is talk radio…no music.

So, I pop in 'West Side Story' and buzz down the freeway listening and signing along to one of my all time favorite Broadway productions. I love Bernstein and the music he directs, and the 'edginess' of his syncopated rhythms really start to lull me into a false sense of calm as I head further south, past the Northfield exit to go east, then further down thru Faribault, then on to my southernmost destination of Owatonna, then hanging a right to go west 12 miles to Waseca.

I already had made arrangements to meet my cousin Desiree at The Mill, the 'new' location for this years' reunion. Guess the 'old' meeting place of the United Methodist Church down by the lake was no longer the place to be. But I had been to this place a few years prior for our 50th high school reunion and enjoyed the atmosphere as well as location. Easy in, easy out, plenty of space… just what a reunion needs.

Since I pulled into Waseca about a half hour early, it gave me a chance to drive around both Clear Lake and Loon Lake and remember back to earlier, happier times in both locations.

And one not so distant caustic memory involving Loon Lake… but that is for another story, another time.

Perhaps.

As I drive around Clear Lake on the east edge of town, I remember back to stories my father and mother would tell me about past times. My grandmother Rathkey working in the hotel up on Maplewood Park doing the cooking; a hotel long since gone and now housing a Boy Scout/Girl Scout building, again, long since usage. But plenty of trails to walk around in, if you like poison ivy and buckthorn nagging at your legs.

Around the lake I would come to Kiesler Campground, owned and run by other relatives and a literal money pit for that family. Camping on one side of the highway and a lake on the other… what a way to make a living! Further on around the bend is Barney's Drive Inn…best rootbeer and burgers in town and a killer view of Clear Lake.

As I continue west on Hwy 14 around the SW corner of the lake I drive past my godparents home, Lee and Bea Rolofson. Though both have since passed, they were both very cordial people and also relatives. Bea's mom, Katrina, was a sister to my maternal grandfather, Warren Scarton, and a lady that lived to a ripe old age before passing on. Stopping at their home as a young boy, just after a run/walk around Clear Lake, was met with cookies, milk, and a game of pool downstairs with 'Uncle Lee'. Always treated me nicely and it was two very sad days when they both passed.

I continue around the lake, going past Thompson's Boat House, another old family haunt that brought back good memories. Now it serves great meals and a frequent place for me to stop by for lunch on my at least 2 yearly trips to Waseca to plant flowers or holiday wreaths at Woodville Cemetery, location of parental and ancestral burial plots.

Wonder if that tradition will have new meanings in the future?

I continue my drive past the church and Clear Lake Park and come up near the Snake Trail, a now-surfaced road that leads to a housing subdivision but was an open field and pasture in my youth. Great streams passing along the lake road my older brothers used to seine for minnows. I think those days are long gone by now.

Finishing up the drive I am now passing the 'rich' people's homes on the east side of the lake, where at one time there were only two homes, then three…with a landing strip running the length of the backyards for Willard Monson's single prop planes. Now you have dentists, bankers, and lawyers living along a 'great view' stretch of land with an exceptional view of the lake and the setting sun every evening.

My short jaunt around the lake brings me back into town on Highway 14 and at the junction of Highway 13 I take a right and head north…past part of the downtown area, past my old homestead in the 600 block, and up past my original home in the 800's block of North State Street. Taking a left brings me to Lau's Meat Market, which today is called Morgan's Meats…great place for sausage, meat cuts, and good conversation, amongst other things. Always a place to stop when in town and since I only get there a few times, a 'must' for bring home and to my sister, Pauline, local food favorites. Their bakery options are second to none, and since both Rindelaub and Preuss Bakeries are long since gone, they fill the need for bread, buns, and dinner rolls. And those homemade cookies never make it home with the original count in the package when I bought it!

A left out of that driveway and a right two blocks later and I am going around Loon Lake, a place dear to my heart from long, long ago. I had classmates that lived around the lake in various homes, and my parents, via my grandparents, had a 3 acre lot on the west end of the lake that had a home we rented out, an old metal fish house that my older brother, Bob, built and left on land (tough fishing there, buddy!), an old out house that made me want to use the 3rd tree on the left rather that go in that spider infested thing, and a dock that provided the best bullhead fishing in the county.

But, with 3 acres of land and trees also comes 3 acres of mowing every two weeks and annual fall raking that usually took several weekends to complete. But the burning of the leaves brought a smell that just can't be duplicated, so the efforts at land management during the spring and summer paid off with simple pleasures as this was usually followed by a weeny roast and perhaps a currant pie my mother would make from the local currant bush. Forget about the mosquito laden raspberry patch…that is a chapter for another horror story from another author!

But after leaving this part of the drive and heading back into town on Highway 14 going east toward The Mill, I am amazed at the calmness that has come over me in the meantime.

Here I was just dreading this drive down to Waseca, meeting Desiree and hearing the news she has to share, and I find myself almost at normal heartbeat anxiously awaiting our reunion. The reason I say 'normal' heartbeat is that I was diagnosed with Afib a few years back…something new but not to me.

I knew my Dad had an irregular heartbeat all his life, and it didn't slow him down one bit. He was an athlete, and a good one; he worked hard and manual labor was nothing new to him. He was robust and active mentally sharp and did not let his heart stop him until his last breath came in the summer of 1996...when his heart finally said 'enough'. He was just shy of 87 years old, and had lived a good life by anyone's standards.

I should be so lucky.

Well, I arrived at The Mill and drove around the far east side where I saw Desiree's AV parked, and she was outside having a cup of coffee. We met, exchanged pleasantries, and went inside her AV for a discussion. Seemed like a logical place to meet, since I didn't want to make a 'scene' inside The Mill should this discussion go south.

And boy, did it go south and in a hurry.

Desiree was not one to mince words, but as calmly and sincerely as possible, with her holding on to my hands as she spoke, simply relayed what her testing had discovered:

From a genetics standpoint, my sister, Pauline and I were not biologically related. The DNA confirmed this, and after conducting three separate tests due to the plethora of sampling material I had sent her including blood, bodily fluids, and hair...and samples of me to compare against...the results were conclusive. She showed me the blood comparison results and what was and what was not possible for genetic agreement.

At least, regarding Pauline and me.

And since our blood types were not of genetic agreement, hence, there could be no possible biological relationship. While these 3 tests were conclusive in regards to the samples sent, there should be more testing done for absolute confirmation of our suspicions.

Since there were no other samples garnered and sent for testing, no other conclusions could be drawn at this point in time. Only that which Desiree had presented to me.

WTF?

I am in absolute shock as to what I just heard, yet trying to stay calm and process everything that Desiree had just shared with me. I am so quiet and still that I just seemed glued to the AV seat, with no intention of moving or getting up to leave. I am just mesmerized by the thought of not being part of this family that things start to happen to my body and are not normal and don't feel 'right'.

I was not having a heart attack, but I am feeling serious constraints around my chest area and more rapid breathing than normal for me, along with some nausea and lightheadedness.

I get up, thank Desiree, and tell her that I need to go and meet up with a friend before processing any more of her information. I let her know I will be in touch, and before leaving, am met with a huge hug lasting way longer than cousins should probably hug each other.

But we both know the impact of what just happened and that the news she had to share would shake me to the core, at the very least.

I go outside and walk around for a few minutes, hoping that the fresh air will help clear my mind and while not take away anything that I just heard, at least let me get my feet back on the ground and try to walk, talk, and act somewhat normal for the duration of the reunion.

People were starting to gather outside The Mill to go inside for the ancestral historical review and business meeting that occurs prior to the other daily activities, and I still wanted to be as involved as possible as there were several relatives I wanted to see and old pictures I wanted to look at.

I had a chance to spend some time reviewing old ancestral pictures and landscapes of former homesteads, and visit for a few minutes with an older cousin, Lori Kanne, an older cousin and mother of a high school friend, Janey Kanne. We have stayed in touch over the years, and with both of us getting closer to the finish line than the starting gate, try to see each other at least yearly on one of my trips to Waseca.

But while we were all seated at various tables throughout The Mill, awaiting the business meeting to start, this feeling in my chest was starting to resurface and my breathing was becoming more labored. I am not one to get sick…I may break things once in awhile, or I may tear things once in awhile, or I may need to have something repaired once in awhile (I have undergone 30 major surgeries over the years), but as a general rule I don't get sick.

Well, this is the day that that rule gets thrown out the window.

I feel like crap and don't want to make a scene in this place with all these relatives around so I gather up my 'stuff' from the back of the room where I am sitting and proceed to pass the registration table and get outside and go straight to my truck.

I manage to throw up before getting in my truck, and as weak as I feel and unstable, pull a really bad Neanderthal move and get in and start up the ignition and drive the 7 blocks on back streets to the Waseca Area Hospital…where I promptly park and staggering, go check myself in through the emergency entrance.

Oh, this day has just gone from bad to worse and I don't know what is going to happen next!

9

HOSPITAL REFLECTIONS

Waseca, Minnesota
July 13, 2024 (later that day)

Like I said earlier, I am not one to get sick, but having to go into a hospital on your own and go through all of the questions and answers they require is a real pain in the ass, if you know what I mean.

Now, don't get me wrong. There were several medical personnel that evidently recognized my family name and I was treated very quickly, very kindly, and with upmost medical professionalism… something you would expect that anyone would get when confronted with a medical situation like the one I was in.

But this was a place I did not want to be; just check me out, tell me what is wrong, and let's get on with things. I still have a couple hours of driving to do and don't plan on calling Julie to tell her of my predicament unless absolutely necessary.

And it was not going to be absolutely necessary to do so!

Well, to make a long story short, after a few hours of testing and probing (I hate probing) and asking questions and checking with other medical records, it was decided that I had indeed suffered (bullshit) a mild panic attack, and that after some rest and medication, I could be discharged and allowed to continue along my way.

All during this time my wife, Julie, thinks I am at the family reunion at The Mill. My older sister, Pauline, thinks I am at the family reunion at The Mill. My older brother, Terry, thinks I am at the family reunion at The Mill. I wanted to be at the family reunion at The Mill.

Well, guess where the hell I am not!?!?!? At The Mill!

I did not want to be in Waseca Memorial Hospital (now the Mayo Clinic Health System) for any longer than necessary. But I have to admit, for a local hospital it really has many things going for it. It was only ½ block from my childhood home on the 600 block of North State Street, and we could be here in less than one minute if necessary.

But today…I just wanted to go home. My ticker was back to its' abnormal rhythm and there was nothing anyone could do to change that. But I needed to get back on the road and head north and back to Crystal and to home and to my wife, Julie.

But I can say that during the time between the testing and probing and final diagnosis and assessments, I was flat on my back in bed with my head propped up looking at puke green walls and thinking:

--- now that Desiree has done her first round of testing, is there anyway that something went wrong and the results were skewed and inaccurate?

Nah…that dog don't hunt.

--- so, if that means what Desiree said it means, does that mean I have an obligation and an immediate mandate to share that information with others?

Well…that dog might hunt.

--- so, if that information should be shared, should it be shared personally in a timely manner or a shotgun approach in one quick email or text?

Oh, hell no…that dog definitely don't hunt.

--- do I tell my immediate family first, or do I tell my siblings first?

Let's let that dog lie for awhile. Let it sleep on it until things are clearer.

Al of these thoughts are now crossing my mind, and trying to keep them in proper context and order and processing arrangement is really tiring.

But there is one central theme that still keeps coming back to me that I have to consider very seriously:

--- do we need more testing information from my siblings and possibly my nuclear family in order to really nail down the lid on this sucker so we are 100% sure of what we are about to announce once the final round of testing is completed?

And…

--- if the answer is 'yes', does this sample gathering and testing need to be done covertly or do we open the whole can of worms now and up front so everyone knows what is going on and why we are doing it?

And while those thoughts are swirling around in my head, I also find myself looking back to the past. Were there other signs or clues that I missed along the way that would have tipped me off that things were 'off' in this household, and that 'this' was not a place where I really 'belonged'?

Man, even at my age now…at 70 years of age…this is a very heavy load to carry around on your shoulders and keep hidden from your family and loved ones. It's almost like trying to live a double life…one side of me wants this and the other side of me wants that.

Talk about a Janus dilemma!

And to top it off…if Desiree's first round of testing is accurate, yet to be proven conclusive, then that means someone or someones knew something way back when and decided to keep it hidden from me and perhaps others until…well, until what we don't know. Perhaps keep it hidden forever unless something or someone came along and…

And started to do some digging!

Nothing stays buried forever….but there had to be…there has to be clues.

But before we get the cart anymore in front of the horse, let's let the dust settle from today and follow up with Desiree next week and plot a course for final resolution.

This quest, this journey, this jaunt into hell as it is turning into has to have more definitive proof in order to validate that which we not only are beginning to believe is the truth but can actually be verified as the truth.

And that means more people are going to be involved, either covertly and on the down low or out in the open for all to see. And the prospects of that option do not sit well with me at this point in time.

I am hurting too much from what has happened thus far to want to openly engage others in the search or even the conversation until all of the cards are on the table for all to see at one final time.

Too many cooks in the kitchen spoil the broth…and this kitchen only has room for two at the present: me and Desiree.

Time for some home cooking…

10

SLEUTHING ... AGAIN

Crystal, Minnesota
Early August, 2024

That drive back home to Crystal from the family reunion in Waseca was one of the longest trips I have ever taken in my life. It was tough keeping up with traffic on 35W going north when my mind wanted to go on the backroads and think about what had transpired less than 12 hours prior.

OK, so I got the information from Desiree, then promptly drove myself to the local hospital where I was diagnosed with a mild panic attack. Several hours later, after convincing the medical team that I was fit to drive back home (upon the threat of checking myself out of the hospital on my own), I made it back to Crystal… worn, shredded of any sense of self worth, and worrying how I was going to hold it together to tell Julie.

Well, lucky for me, Julie had left me a note on the great room kitchen counter indicating she was in Maple Grove with her sister and brother in law at their condo playing games and I should give her a call when I got in, if it wasn't too late. I proceeded to do just that, sounding like 'good old Donny' and got in the truck for the drive northwest to go pick her up.

Julie could tell something was wrong on the drive home, but I told her it was a combination of some bad sushi at lunch along with eating some pulled pork way too fast at a local diner in Faribault on my way home. Story bought, we got home and immediately got ready for bed. Sleep could not come fast enough for me after the grueling day I had, so I rolled on my right side after a good night kiss and tried to hit 'deep sleep'.

That lasted about 5 minutes…then lay awake for hours thinking. I could not shut down…shut down…have to shut down.

Shut down…

And out.

When I awoke the next morning I realized that I needed some time to decompress from what had just happened so I planned a pre-archery hunting exploration trip out to west central Minnesota where our oldest daughter, Tristan, and her family live. This is where I archery and firearms hunt, and this time of year was about one month out from the start of the archery season…a perfect time for tree pruning, putting out scent and mineral attractants, and getting the deer blinds ready for Grandpa to go sit in.

Ever since 2016, when I had a bad fall and subsequent surgery on my left lower leg and ankle area, I have hunted from the ground based on medical advice and personal decisions to stay alive. While I prefer to take a shot, archery or firearms, from a higher angle, which allows for a higher entry point and lower exit point for better blood drainage, I have sacrificed that option for a more direct line of fire done on a horizontal plane. I just need to be accurate and aim for certain organs rather that just let one fly!

My two weeks out in the woods area and being with Tristan's family was just the rejuvenation I needed to get my head back in the game and pursue the next tasks that Desiree had laid out for me in our most recent phone call of a few days ago.

It made no sense to try and obtain any DNA samples from my wife, Julie, or either of our two daughters, Tristan and Cynthia, as they had nothing to do with the DNA question that was still unsolved. They were of a different generation and combination process, one that was not in question.

The same held true for our five grandchildren, who by now ranged in age from young teenager to college senior. Their DNA did not enter into the equation so I need not spend any time in this arena.

But Desiree did tell me that in order to have definitive proof that could not be repudiated, I should get a DNA sample from each of my parents and older brother, Terry.

Well, since my father passed in 1996 and my mother two years later in 1998, that seemed like a very tall order right out of the shoot. But then it dawned on me that I did have samples of all their DNA, although they would be 'secondary' in nature to something like a direct blood draw.

I called Desiree, told her what I had in my possession already, and considering the fact that we still didn't want to tip off any other relatives as to what was going on behind the scenes, Desiree told me that the secondary DNA samples could work out just fine with their modern testing equipment, but gave me specific instructions on securing and packing for the Fed Ex shipment back out to Oregon.

I got back home, unpacked, shared pleasantries with Julie… and devised my plan to secure the additional DNA samples for testing.

First of all, my older brother, Terry, who had visited just a few months back along with his wife, Tania, had left me a bright red Cabela's jacket as an early birthday present. It was the jacket that he had worn for the previous several years, but had gotten too big for him to wear, so he was very willing to 'share'…of his own volition…this valuable item with his younger brother, not knowing the real value in such an acquisition.

This jacket would hold a ton of DNA bodily fluid and sweat

samples for testing and since we 'knew' that he and Pauline were biological brother and sister, this should help clinch the deal as far as my position was concerned.

Now, as for my mother and father, this was going to be even easier. The spring, 1998 night my mother passed away at Lake Shore Inn Nursing Home in Waseca, I was present by her bedside. I was the only one present at the time, as my sister had just taken a few minutes break and was down the hall getting something to eat. It was late at night, with very few shift personnel working.

But within a few minutes of her passing, the charge nurse lifted Mom's head and took off an Eastern Star necklace that she had always worn around her neck, and gave it to me in a little baggie. While I appreciated the gesture at the time, I would not realize the real value of that moment until now, knowing that I kept that necklace in that same baggie for all of the past 26 years in the jewelry box that sits on top of my dresser.

That necklace would hold my mothers DNA all of these years…undisturbed and ready for testing and analysis…as a secondary source of direct DNA collection.

That just left my Dad.

But that turned out to be the easiest.

Downstairs in my basement office area in our Crystal home, sitting right there in front of me on a file cabinet is an old pipe holder and glass tobacco cannister…still holding 6 pipes that not only were used by my father, Leon, but 2 that were used by my paternal grandfather Hans and never used by my father as the bite was not adjusted right for his mouth.

I hit the mother load when it came to Dad's DNA. It would be all over the pipe handle and most assuredly on the pipe stem and bite. Desiree indicated that her testing equipment could easily breakdown the crystalized bodily fluid/saliva on the mouthpiece and convert it into appropriate DNA testing material in a matter of days.

No need to send any of the tobacco, though I know for a fact that it has been in that glass container ever since Dad's passing in 1996. It is not unusual for me to sit down at my desk, or when coming downstairs to do other work or get dressed for hunting, to take the wooden top off the container, breathe in a huge vapor of the still pungent tobacco, and think back to happier times with Dad.

Now, that memory will never pass, no matter what the damn testing indicates.

So, just like before, I package up the items individually and get them ready for the Fed Ex store in Maple Grove. Luckily, I have a few grocery errands to run for Julie so I can slip out of the house, get this package into the truck, and be off and on my way with none the wiser. Overnight shipping, this time about $119, and Desiree will have this in her hands, ready to process in two days at her Oregon lab.

So by now, in late August, I have gotten the first round of DNA testing information and gathered samples to have tested in round two. No one within my nuclear family knows what is going on and suspects nothing. I have remained as cool, calm, and collected as I can be and no one suspects the wiser.

But that trip back to Waseca started to stir some very dormant memories from the past, and my concerns were that some of those memories were coming home to roost for what may be the first… and final…time.

All actions have consequences…some are good….some are not.

But all negative actions and consequences must be accounted for. One must be held accountable, if not to an authority within, or an authority on earth, then the higher authority we all have to stand in front of some day.

Wby do I have this feeling of foreboding that there is a consequence with my name written all over it that will come back and slap me upside the head right when I don't want it to happen? I thought that action was long since buried and out of my memory banks. But I guess that is not to be.

A person with my memory talents never forgets anything.

Ever.

And that is where the real danger lies.

Just ahead…

For the 'dark' side of Donny that usually lies dormant can, at the snap of a finger and in the blink of an eye, become dominant and overtake all common sense and rationalization thoughts that one might have had buried for all these years.

Driving down to Waseca awakens those old haunting memories.

Driving past Central High School, specifically the southside playground area, awakens those old haunting memories.

And then there is the reality of the present, and the now, and the responsible actions that a person of Donny's stature and position should uphold and adhere to for the 'good' of character.

I was always taught that 'if a man's word is no good, then his signature on a sheet of paper was no good also'. That came from a story my father would tell about my grandfather upon the latter's visit to one of the local banks in search of a 30 day loan for his implement business. The newly hired banker, not knowing grandpa, wanted his signature on a document promising payback within the 30 day loan period.

I think my grandfather's response provided a great life lesson, as that initial banker was fired within 15 minutes of my grandfather walking out of the bank, walking 50 yards down Main Street to another bank, and walking away with the loan based on a handshake and his word.

For the record, the loan was paid back within 2 weeks, solidifying the Rathkey name again in the business annals of Waseca County…forever.

Please, Donny…don't screw this up and let several generations of a good name go down the drain because of your old grudges and a revenge-based heart.

Please…

II

UPPER ELEMENTARY REFLECTIONS

Waseca, Minnesota
1961-1965

Looking back on some younger days in elementary school and life in general, I am struck with one very distinct definitive:

There are two unlimited constants in the world: one is the universe and the second is the stupidity of humankind.

Since I don't know much about the former but am an expert on the latter, like Samuel Clemons/Mark Twain indicated….'write what you know'.

I know that my middle and upper elementary school years and time at home was an absolute terror for people on both ends of that experience. I don't know if my mischievous behaviors led to discipline and punishment, or if because of the discipline and punishment I became immune to such endeavors and continued along a path of self destruction and naughtiness simple because of the following fact:

I could.

Yes, I was aware of the 'things' that I was doing and that if found out (not when, but if) there would be some sort of repercussions that were not in my best interest, either mentally, psychologically, spiritually, or physically.

Especially the physical part.

It's not that I was becoming immune to pain and suffering, it was just that I knew it was going to be coming but I seemed to have no definitive control to prevent the actions I caused from happening. I was becoming aware of the special 'abilities' I had of the recognition and recall nature, but that was of little consolation to me when I was getting my butt spanked or my upper arms grabbed with nails embedded in my skin deep enough to cause immediate bleeding and bruising for days to come.

It was during these 4 years, grades 3-6, that I really started to act out and misbehave to the point that not only was I not doing well in school but I was not doing well out of school, at home, playing with other kids, etc.

I was just not a little person that others wanted to be around.

Oh, don't get me wrong. I had my moments. I had plenty of those. I could be the most charming little angel you ever laid eyes on while at the same time I am picking your pocket, stealing from your school desk, or pissing on the plants in your garden.

Things just happened and consequences be damned. But looking back I am still looking for clues that something was wrong, something was out of place, something within this grouping does not belong here…and it was always me.

But what were my behaviors that my older brothers and sister did not exhibit that seemed to be second nature to me? Why was I:

--- stealing from other student's desks, looking for 'full' pencils that I did not have? Miss. Henry was not pleased with that one.

--- taking another kids marbles when I had a leather pouch full of them myself? Miss Tankley gave me a very dirty look when confronting me on this one.

--- going into the faculty bathroom due to an 'emergency' in the hallway, but picking up the discarded lunch tickets the teacher had just thrown away and selling them back to students for $.10 when we paid $.25 in the first place for a daily lunch? Damn that Miss Fernby!

--- using a Bic pen to mark up my new social studies book, but tell the teacher it came that way when confronted with it in front of the entire class? Same Miss Fernby!

--- sliding down the hill by the baseball park on my way home on my math book, because it provided more traction on the ice, then telling the teacher a dog ran off with the book and damaged it before I could get it back? Miss Fell really let my parents have it come conference time for this move!

--- going into the classroom during lunchtime to retrieve some confiscated marbles the teacher had put in the fish aquarium, but leaving water marks that led back to the pouch in my desk? And I really liked Mrs. Deerfield…she was the best…until this.

--- sneaking back into our home, taking money from our housekeeper, Mrs. Olstein, from the purse in her downstairs bedroom, and use it at the local bakery downtown for brownies? Guess my footprints coming in from the rain gave me away.

--- cutting the silver beaver off of the ribbon holding it from a scouting momento my troop-leader father was awarded and selling it for a dime to the Fennert kid at the other end of the block that wanted it for scouting. Really dumb, Donny…

--- taking money (dollar or two at a time) from the bi-monthly envelop that my mother kept in the laundry room table (that was my father's paycheck) to use for 'goodies' that other kids had and that I didn't. Mom never told Dad about this indiscretion as far as I know. Wish she had…I had a spanking coming for that one.

---but why stop at my father's pay envelope? Why not also take money from my sister's fruit money envelope located in the same place on the same table? Pauline would earn money from picking raspberries out at the 3 acres and then selling them to local grocery stores and friends of the family. But wait a minute…I also picked those same damn raspberries in the mosquito-laden, steaming hot afternoons…and got nothing!

--- but one that really hurt me was having the head football coaches' daughter, Dawn Milton, ride by me on her bike on her way home in late spring and call me a bad word as she passed me. I stopped walking, glanced down, picked up a small rock, and threw it in the air as if I was trying to hit a mallard in flight. I could not duplicate that throw in a million years…it arced up and came right down on Dawn's head when she was about 30 yards from me and going away, and hit her smack dab on the top of her noggin. I heard the howl and the scream and saw her pick up the speed on her bicycle. I don't even think she stopped for traffic when she crossed Highway 13 and went one more block, living only 1 block from our home on North State Street. But I guess things never got reported back to my parents as I never heard about it again, except for Dawn sticking her tongue out at me in school the next day and rubbing the white bandage on her head. I heard later on that that was the evening old Coach Milton had to tell his wife that he was having an affair with the wife of an assistant football coach and fellow teacher at school. Never did see Dawn again after that school year ended.

--- playing marbles with a neighbor boy at his house at the other end of the block, and then stealing his prize 'shooter; and running home when he went inside his home to go to the bathroom. Ended up taking it back 30 minutes later when his mom called mine…caught red handed. And these were friends of my parents…damn.

--- walking up to the Standard Oil station a block south of our home, going inside and waiting for the owner/proprietor to go outside and service a vehicle, then sneak around his counter and grab some change from the candy box to get some pop and candy.

Wonder if that gave him the 'right' to feel me up in my chest later on? Mr. Brisbane was not a man to be trifled with, I guess.

--- sneaking into the old fire station where my Dad worked, on his day off, catching his fellow shift partner, Larry Napberg, taking a nap with his back to me, and me going into his locker and taking out some change from the top shelf that he left in a band-aid container. I was really quiet…but didn't realize that his 'nap' was only a ruse and that he was watching me all the time from a mirror on the wall on the opposite side of the room. He just turned and looked at me, said nothing, and lay back down. I would repeat that same behavior years later when working at Corcoran's Industrial Plant during a winter break, only this time it was from a fellow worker, Finn O'reilly. Funny looking back on this situation…I was the only one in the plant in the assembly room at the time of my heist.

Or was I?

I could go on and on, but you get the drift by now that I was not in the running for 'Boy of the Year' in any of my elementary school years. And the 'mistakes' I was making were not so much mistakes as they were 'choices'.

I still believe that idiom to this day: there are mistakes, of which there are two kinds, and there are choices. 'Mistakes of the head' we all make every day and usually without much consequence… something got left out, something got missed, we forgot to do something, etc. Those mistakes are easily made and easily forgotten or forgiven.

There are also 'mistakes of the heart'…choices that were often intentionally made that hurt others or ourself and usually resulted in people not being as forgiving or forgetting as before. These are the mistakes that are the most deadly and serious.

And then there are choices: you see Door A and Door B. You know what lies behind each door and you purposely chose the one you should now go through. Some people would consider this a mistake of the heart, for you usually know ahead of time when bad things can and will happen, but I am not going to split hairs over semantics.

But I am able to look back and see that behaviors I exhibited were completely foreign to my parents, for they did not have to deal with any of these behaviors from my older brothers and sister. My older brothers were absolute role models both in school and outside of school, in the community and in church and in life in general. Waseca was a better place because of the Rathkey boys; well, at least the older two.

And my sister, being the only girl in the family, meant she got everything a girl needed first…she was the only girl. No hand me downs, no second hand clothes or toys. But when it came to Donny, well, that was another thing…

I wish I had been given some of the hand me downs that I found later on in my brothers closets, like jeans and sweaters and shirts that I could have and would have worn in my older years. But no, no, no…Donny didn't get just a few hand me downs from his older brothers, he got hand me downs from his older sister!

Yes…blue shorts with a bunny stitched into the side where I had to wear a longer tee shirt to try and cover up that damn bunny from being seen by other boys when we got together to play baseball or kick the can or some other neighborhood game.

And the teasing continued. And so did the misbehaviors.

And in the fall, wearing an old pair of 'kickareenos' that were my sister's…a low cut boot/shoe with sides that folded up with warmer material…clearly a ladies winter boot. But no…this is what Donny had to wear if he was going to go outside and play with neighborhood kids.

And the teasing continued. And so did the misbehaviors.

It got to the point where by the end of the 6th grade, my time at Hartley Elementary was a blessing in disguise. Gone would be the days when I had to try and slink home after school by dodging in and out of the pine tree line just west of the school and before you got to the football field, 'cause I had pissed off some high schoolers that drove home that way and I was always swearing at them and flipping them off. But I had to time my exit from school just right to either beat them up the street past the ballpark or wait until I thought they had driven by and then proceed west.

But I guess picking up that rock and throwing it at their car as it drove by wasn't the smartest thing I had ever done. At least, not according to my father when he had to explain to Mr. Biermann that I was simply reacting to what his older son had done by tormenting me in trying to get home from school. Since I was not on an allowance at any time in my elementary or high school years, I guess Dad paid to have the broken car window replaced, and it would have come out of his paycheck.

But, damn…to take out a window of a moving vehicle means that there may be a pitcher's role for me somewhere down the line!

If I can make it that far!

But as I conclude looking back and remembering these early years in my life, I keep looking for more clues about did I or did I not belong? Was there at least one thing that I could remember that would help me sort out this confusion that I was experiencing?

And then it came to me.

Clear as a sheet of ice, hard as a bell, and sticking to my memory like warm, freshly-baked cinnamon rolls.

The incident at home with my mother.

I was just completing 4th grade, having brought home a small potholder made in Miss Fell's classroom, one that I had handmade on a loom as an individual class art project. I knew it was 4th grade, because when directions were given to bring to school a skein of yarn, my mother had instead opted to buy a smaller, cheaper size of yarn. As a result, when making my potholder in class, I ran out of yarn due to the lack of material and had to splice another color from her pile of leftover material in order to finish my project. Purple and pink do not go well together when you are a boy.

Hell…purple and pink do not go well together when you are anybody!

As a result, I got home and was in a pissed off mood, even for a 4th grader. And for whatever reason, decided that the ceiling fan should be turned on just for the heck of it. Litle did I know that my mother had spent part of her morning tiding up around the fireplace…which was just below said ceiling fan…and when the fan went on, so did the ashes that had been scooped up but not removed from the fireplace grate area.

I had just done something terribly wrong and the only thing I could think of was to lie on the floor and wait for hell to come around the corner and swallow me up.

She did.

After shutting off the fan, she looked down at me, and said; 'you know what happens to bad boys?'

And she drew her right hand across her throat in a slashing motion, enlarged her eyes, stared at me, and then turned and walked away.

I could not recall ever being so scared as I was at that moment. That was the first time…the very first time…that I really questioned who I was, where I was, why I was there, and what was going to happen to me. Especially when my father got home.

To the best of my knowledge, Dad never knew about that situation. The ashes were cleaned up, nothing more was said between me and my mother, and I went to bed early that evening and sang myself to sleep…something that was quite common back in the day. At least until my sister came into the room and got in her bed, as we shared a bedroom till she graduated in 1965 and went on to college at the U of M.

But that slashing motion across her neck and the bulging of her eyes was only a precursor to things that were to come.

If you thought my elementary years were tough, that was only the beginning of what I was capable of.

But again, the question was and has to be: why is this piece of the family puzzle so unlike the other pieces?

We know that my sister and I are not biologically related.

We assume that my brothers and sister are biologically related.

We assume that my parents and my brothers and sister are biologically related.

So…by deduction, and hopefully further testing and analysis, we can ascertain if I am biologically related to my parents and if not…

Where did I come from?

Who did I come from?

Why am I here, in this family, and not in my own?

And who knew about this and when did they know it?

Who? What? Where? When? Why?

Only time will tell, and that time is almost up.

Time to buckle up, strap in, and put on your big boy pants, 'cause

Things are going to get somewhat dicey from here on in!

12

OH, CRAP...

Crystal, Minnesota
October, 2024

Waiting for a call from Desiree is getting to be like waiting for a kidney stone to pass. You want it to happen, you want it to happen now, you want it to happen painlessly, but at the same time, you would like that cup to pass from you.

Sorry...couldn't resist the analogy. Sorry, Jesus.

Anyway, I am home, downstairs at my desk, working on some hunting blind-placement plans when the phone rings. The caller is from Oregon, and I know that it is not from a Ducks fan wanting to sell me tickets to the upcoming Rose Bowl.

I grab the receiver and all I can do is listen while Desiree shares what she has to tell me. I ask a few clarification questions, thank her for her efforts, and tell her I await the return of the testing samples, or what is left of them, at her earliest convenience. I let her know I will contact her within a few days after my mind has digested what she just told me. We leave each other cordially and in good spirits.

Good spirits, my ass!

I was just told that she and her testing team have processed the sampling materials I sent to her...the necklace of my mother's, the pipes of my father and grandfather, and the jacket from my brother...and the results were conclusive and definitive:

According to the most recent DNA testing analysis possible, first of all, I am not the biological brother of my older sibling, Terry. This really didn't come as a surprise, since it was already documented and verified that I am not the biological brother of my older sister, Pauline.

But still, to hear it, sucks.

The next part of the conversation stung more, but again, was not totally out of the realm of possibility when I sent in the samples for testing in the first place. Desiree indicated that from strictly a DNA standpoint, and DNA does not lie...I am not the biological son of Leon and Irma Rathkey, nor am I the grandson of paternal grandfather Hans Johann Rathkey.

Desiree went on to explain to me, in layman's terms, the scientific reasoning behind her analysis based on the samples she tested. What it boils down to is this:

--- there are basically 4 major, definitive blood types: O A B and AB

--- when you 'add' or factor in the Rh factor into each of the blood types, you actually end up with 8 different blood types in totality: O (+ and -); A (+ and -); B (+ and -) and AB (+ and -). The (+) stands for 'positive' and the (-) stands for negative Rh factors. This compatibility factor was introduced in 1968 and has been a constant mainstay in all biological blood work and analysis done worldwide in over the past 50 years. The basis of the Rh factor deals with maternal immune systems and whether or not people with incompatible blood types can or should have children, but also lends credence to blood transfusions as to whether or not the recipient is 'eligible' for a donor's blood to be given to him or her in a medical emergency.

So, for someone, like my mother who has A+ blood and my father who has AB+ blood, when you factor in blood grouping, blood type matching, blood type antibodies and blood types and antigens, you find yourself looking at children with compatible blood types to that combination.

My sister, Pauline, has blood type A+: perfectly compatible and a match to her parents.

My brother, Terry, has blood type AB+: perfectly compatible and a match to his parents.

I have blood type A-: I am not a match to the union of those two adult parents. Neither am I a match individually to either one of those two adult parents.

The continued analysis of the skin samples and a single drop of dried blood on the Eastern Star necklace of my mother that was sent in for analysis further verified that which I have already stated: her DNA on that sample did not match my DNA sample that Desiree had on record in her Oregon lab.

Neither did the sweat analysis from the jacket of my brother offer any DNA proof other than he and Pauline are biological siblings, while there was no match to me.

The pipes from my father Leon and grandfather Hans simply sealed the deal, as long since hardened DNA samples from the stem and mouth bite indicated that which we already surmised: while there was a DNA match with both my older brother and sister to my father and grandfather, there was no DNA match with me from the pipe samples taken for analysis.

As the vaudeville comedy team of Laurel and Hardy would say, usually very often:

"Well. This is another fine mess you've gotten me into'.

Being given and being able to understand scientific data is a point of strength in my wheelhouse. When I was younger I often thought of majoring in some field of science, perhaps biology, as I was fascinated by the wonders of that world. But organic chemistry and I had a falling out in college and my major shifted faster than a buck dismounting a doe in heat during breeding season in the Minnesota woods!

But, again, being given the data, understanding its' meaning, and then having to digest what it all means is a totally different animal. I was now really caught in a headwind that I was having a hard time navigating, both physically, mentally, and emotionally.

Now that I had the information, and that information was not going to change no matter how hard I wished for it to be so, I had to stop and think before proceeding with a plan. I could not just sit on this information and go on with my life as if nothing had happened the past 7 months. I had invested too much in getting to this point in time that I needed to sit and contemplate what the next move(s) could and should be, not just for me but for those around me that will be directly affected by this information and the resulting actions taken.

Oh, this is gonna take some time. Time that I don't have to wait for.

And this is gonna hurt in more ways than one. But I have to go thru this pain.

But the questions that have to be asked now are more important than the ones already asked and answered.

Who? What? Where? When? How?

And most importantly...WHY?

13

THINK!

Crystal, Minnesota
November-December, 2024

Who?
What?
Where?
When?
How?
Why?

These were the six questions that had been gnawing at me for the previous many months since my last and most eviscerating phone call from Desiree. It was like my world was not only turned upside down and inside out, but it was if I was off in a cloud somewhere, looking down and watching all of this happen.

My fall, which was usually joyous routines of archery and firearms hunting, either alone or with family, continued to happen, but with less enthusiasm than I would normally show. Yes, my son in law, JimBob, got a nice buck opening day as did my youngest grandson, Cody. A really nice, first time buck that put the rest of us to shame, well, at least it put Grandpa to shame: I ended up taking a small nubbin buck that happened to come by my groundblind and I decided I needed to get in on the action so my older grandsons had some good protein in their college apartment freezers.

In hindsight, I think I shot that small deer out of frustration as I was thinking about the past and not concentrating on the present and looking forward to the future...whatever that may hold. Remember, up to this point…and beyond…no one but Desiree knows of what I was up to or the results that I had found.

But that secret could not be kept in the dark forever…or could it? What would be gained or lost by digging more and finding out more of the answers to the basic six questions that lay in front of me?

If, indeed, it was not too late to find out such answers?

All fall and early winter I kept racking my brain trying to find answers to questions I held in isolation of hard, factual data…all I had were theories, wild ideas, nightmares. I needed to make a plan that would either lead me to a dead end, or to the answers that so far had eluded me and my mental thoughts about them.

I needed to search all material present for any clues that may lead me in the direction I needed to go to find out the truth. Remember what Dad always said: 'when you have the opportunity to do so, you always set the record straight.'

But while not a man to swear, one of his most favorite sayings was 'why does there seem to be so many more horses asses than horses?' And I am at that point of believing him.

But after fall and winter reflections and spending time with my family, at least as much as we could over the holidays and with them both living some distance from Julie and me, I decided to put pen to paper and devise a plan, a logical forthright plan, that would take me from where I was to where I needed and wanted to be, and gathering the pertinent information that was necessary along the way to answer the one basic question that would gnaw at me until my death, unless addressed:

WHO WAS I? WHO AM I?
WHERE, AND FROM WHOM, DID I COME FROM?
AND WHO OR WHOM PLOTTED THIS DECEPTION
FROM THE START?

My six original questions were still in the mix, and they would entertain me promptly over the next several months, for I knew that while I had a wealth of 'family' information here in Crystal in old family historical documents and chests and books…it was not MY family!

And this was the hard part coming to grips with.

This was someone else's family that I, for whatever reason or reasons, became a part of but it was just that…a 'part' but not 'part of the whole'. It's like being on a team but being the benchwarmer. Or being in the group but always bringing up the rear.

You're there…but in the same sense, you're not.

But while those six original questions were front and foremost in my thinking, I now had to entertain the additional three major questions that dealt more with actual history and possibly nefarious deception than the others.

And I also had to deal with reality. After thinking long and hard about my next steps, I realized that I could no longer do it on my own, but I needed help. Not necessarily help in the sense of having other people know of my present situation and information already found, but help in the sense of pointing me in the right direction so that I could uncover other pieces of information that while seemingly unimportant on the surface, once threaded together would finally tell the full story of my origination, my lineage, and how I arrived on the scene in this particular situation.

That means I needed to go to Waseca, as a starting place, and start at the very beginning. I needed to go back in time to when Irma Rathkey became pregnant, during the time of pregnancy, and finally to the hospital the morning of October 6, 1953…the recorded date of my birth.

But, wait…this is not the 'family' that I am looking for. I need to go deeper into whatever records and archives I could find to ascertain the 'rest of the story', as Paul Harvey would say. I need to scour whatever pieces of paper were still available after over 70 years, and Lord know where they were located and in whos' possession or guardianship.

And with me being over 70 years old, now 71, with most if not all of my 'relevant' relatives already passed or significantly older than me, who could I turn to for any insight as to the potential accuracy of what I needed to find?

But I had to find out. I had to try.

But as Yoda would say in Star Wars movie: 'Do, or Do Not. There is no Try.'

Damn that shriveled up, old, little Jedi Warrior…always right and always on point!

But I also realized that the finality was not my birth…that was the beginning.

But if this was the beginning of my birth…whos' finality was it?

I see birth laying ahead.

I also see death.

Research would reveal one innocently aided by others.

Memory would reveal one deliberately sanctioned by me.

Which one would survive the journey?

14

START DIGGING

Waseca, Minnesota
January 2025

The only place that I can think of, outside of the family historical documents and items that I have in our Crystal home cedar chest and upstairs secretary, would be in Waseca…somewhere, someplace. But where?

I have always been a change agent in my professional career, first as a high school social studies teacher and football/wrestling/track coach, then later on as an assistant principal, principal, assistant superintendent, superintendent, and private sector administrator. That means change to me is 'normal' and 'usual' as long as it is well thought out, planned down to the most minute detail, and logically formatted to take into all accounts considerations from affected parties.

Why would this research endeavor be any different? All of the factors and elements that I used in the workforce need to come together and be in play in order for this undertaking to be successful. I need to know who I am and where I came from, and I need to start at the beginning.

In Waseca.

I take a few days to formulate a plan based on logic and sequential algorithms, then backtrack it to the past to plot a path of finding out what I need to know. I know that with my documented birthdate of October 6, 1953, at 7:26 am at Waseca Memorial Hospital, as signed by Dr. Cecil Hampton and sworn to the Clerk of Court, Waseca County, on October 15, 1953, that this is a starting point. At least for 'part' of the starting.

With a birthdate of October 6th, and estimating the general gestation period for a normal female at that time in history, my mother became pregnant around New Year's Day, or shortly thereafter, 1953.

Must have been a hell of a New Year's party, that's all I can say!

But one must consider that other biological factors may have entered the picture, such as the 'advanced' age of my mother at my birth. Mom was born in 1915, already had three children in 1937, 1941, and 1947, and then I come along in 1953…to someone. That means by accepted records on file, my mother was 38 years old at the time of my birth…somewhat getting 'up there' per most scales. And my father, born in 1909, would have been 44 years old. Again, getting 'up there' but not totally out of line for a man at that period in time.

Now…that is what the 'official' record would say about things at that time. But we know differently. We know better.

We now know the 'truth' based on incontrovertible DNA proof. Neither of these people were my biological parents.

So….what happened? This is where the search has to begin.

My initial trips to Waseca during January were based on lies to my wife in that I was checking up on some 'older' relatives and since there are so few of us left on that branch of the 'Rathkey' and 'Scarton' tree, it was not a hard sell. The only thing I don't like, especially in older years, is winter driving, so I kept my trips to Waseca as minimal as possible as to timing, but maximization of my time once I was there.

I knew I needed to start at the County Court House, located just two blocks south of our home on North State Street. I was very comfortable talking with the Clerk of Court and going over historical records as I often used their offices when checking out 'old' property lines from the past relative to where my ancestors settled, farmed, and started their immigrant lives here in America.

But the Court House can only house so many records of the nature that I needed, so I was sent across the street to the County Court House Annex, which was a remodeled Ben Franklin from my high school days and even before that, the Waseca Hotel which burned down in the early '60's. The records attendant happened to be an old high school classmate, Barb Matzen, and she was most helpful in directing me to archival material that proved to be the very 'pot of gold' that I was looking for.

It seems that on October 6th, 1953, during the night and very early pre-dawn hours, there was a terrific wind and rain storm that hit Waseca and the surrounding areas. It lasted for hours and knocked out power to most of the town, and downed power lines and trees only delayed partial functioning of the electrical grid for several days. You gotta remember, this was the '50's…things were not set up for speed or recovery like they are today.

Things moved slowly and with deliberate actions…and also helped cover items under the cloak of darkness that should have remained hidden.

Well, it seems that according to the archival records of the hospital that around 5:00 am that morning Irma Rathkey, accompanied by her husband, Leon, arrived at the now almost blacked-out hospital, as Mrs. Rathkey was obviously pregnant and about to give birth as she was in the early throes of labor.

Since the usual birthing room located on the first floor of the hospital was without power and functioning capabilities, Mrs. Rathkey was taken to the 2nd floor into a semi private room, awaiting the arrival of Dr. Hampton, who was anticipated within the hour. Mrs. Bathke was in extreme distress during this time, and was given a sedative and later on a dose of morphine to help calm her down and alleviate some of the labor pains, that were increasing though no dilation of the birth canal nor crowning of the fetus was evident. This initial shot and subsequent IV was administered by Doris Splitter, Dr. Hampton's personal nurse and the only nurse available at that time of the early morning due to transportation issues revolving around the existing storm outside.

Mrs. Rathkey soon slipped into a more relaxed mode of rest and within the hour was totally unresponsive to what was going on around her. She was not in a coma state, but was so relaxed by the pain relieving morphine that she had simply slipped into a deep REM sleep mode and oblivious to her surroundings.

At about the same time, according to the records, a second young woman was brought into the hospital…actually, stumbled in through the front door without any assistance or escort…and was obviously pregnant and also in a state of soon to be delivery. This woman was simply identified as 'Jane Doe' on the medical records as she carried with her no identification, no identifying markings or jewelry, and no medical insurance information. She was simply a 'walk-in' off the street.

But a 'walk in' at 5:45 am on a storm-filled morning, with no escort?

Jane Doe was directed by an attendant to the same second floor room that Mrs. Rathkey was in and given the second, available bed so that both pregnant ladies were within earshot of each other in the same room in the same ward, and just across the hall from what would become the 'emergency surgery center' for the next several hours. Mr. Rathkey, after escorting his wife to her hospital room, was guided back downstairs to the 'men's waiting room', a common room back in the day for expectant fathers, located just outside the viewing room for newborn babies. Leon was allowed to smoke his pipe and just sit and wait, like all expectant fathers do!

Dr. Hampton arrived shortly after 6:45 am and was directed to the room where the two ladies, and Doris Splitter, were in attendance. After checking on Mrs. Rathkey, according to the official records, Dr. Hampton began a preliminary examination of his 'new' patient, as there were no other physicians or delivery personnel available for assistance.

This new, young mother to be was estimated to be around 16 years of age, according to records, and was in severe distress due to pain in her abdomen. Dr. Hampton was able to discern that this was the girl's first pregnancy and distress prior to full labor was not uncommon. She was given a sedative by Doris Splitter to help her relax, and a small IV dosage of morphine for the pain of pre-labor. She drifted off to sleep and was soon as docile as Mrs. Rathkey, lying in the other bed with the same symptoms.

Dr. Hampton ascertained that both births would be almost simultaneously dealt with within the upcoming hour, so he went down to the physician's locker room to change into appropriate medical clothing to take charge of the deliveries. Other medical assistance personnel were expected to arrive, pending transportation issues due to the storm, within the hour, as a shift change was due around 7am for the hospital in general.

At 7:20 am, Dr. Hampton was summoned back to the birthing room presently occupied by Mrs. Rathkey and Jane Doe. Mrs. Rathkey, still under due to the IV medical drip, was crowning and birth was imminent. In the other bed, Jane Doe was also still under due to the morphine drip and was also beginning to crown. Doris Splitter was in the room, and then a scream was heard down the hallway.

An intern nursing assistant from the high school, who had come in to assist in whatever manner she could during this time of calamity due to the storm, came across Judge Noolen doubled over in the main hallway, complaining of lower abdomen pain and almost delirious due the pain. She put him in a wheelchair, brought him to second floor immediately as the first floor surgical suite was still without power, and directed to proceed to the room two rooms down and to the east from the birthing room presently occupied by Mrs. Rathkey and Jane Doe.

Dr. Hampton and his nurse, Doris Splitter, left the birthing room to attend to Judge Noolen and ascertained within minutes that his gall bladder was about to rupture and needed immediate surgery to not only remove the gall bladder, but save his life. But without adequate medical personnel present, the operation that should be routine at best will now become a medical emergency as only a few hands will be available to attend to the needs that many hands would normally be accounted for to do.

Back in the birthing room, a newly born baby girl…stillborn… deformed and barely recognizable, was wrapped in a blanket and placed at the end of the bed on a presentation table. Her mother, still sleeping and unaware of her surroundings, would not awaken for a few more minutes.

A few minutes later another baby, a baby boy…healthy and screaming his lungs out…would be quickly delivered, wrapped in a blanket and placed at the end of the bed on another presentation table. He, too, had a mother that was unaware of her surroundings, but it was not due to the morphine IV drip in her arm or the sedative shot that was given to her prior to that.

She was unaware of her surroundings because she was physically unaware…

She was resting in the sweet slumber of eternal rest that can come after a long life of trials and tribulations, or can come after a short life filled with despair and disappointment.

Or it can come after an internal uterus bleed that could not be stopped in time…

There was no one there to identify the situation.

There was no one there to stop it in time.
There was just no one there that could do anything.
Except for her…
She had to do something…
And quickly!

15

FAMILY SECRETS

Crystal and Waseca, Minnesota
February, 2025

There is an old joke about three people can keep a secret if two of them are dead. Well, there is a reason why the word is 'secret' because it implies something that is to be and/or remain hidden from view or knowledge of others.

But secrets that are family secrets can often times be destructive if left hidden for too long, or forever, and not brought out into the light of day for full exposure. People hide things for many reasons, such as being ashamed, being scared, being unaware of unintended consequences…the list can go on and on.

And it is usually thought that the item or factual point that is the object of the hidden secret is best kept under wraps so that others don't get 'hurt' by the knowledge of what it contains.

I get it. I understand the premise.

But when a person's past, or their future, hinge on the truth… doesn't that account for something? Doesn't that account for the truth being laid bare for all to view and then decide how to react?

I don't know. I don't have either the correct or the definitive answer as to the validity of the statement. And I am sure not in a position to play God and be judge, jury, and executioner relative to another person's deeds or misdeeds.

(Strike that last comment. This will come back to haunt me and be fully explained to you in an upcoming chapter, so hold that thought and we will come back to it later.)

Where this is all streaming from is that during my research trips to Waseca earlier this year I came across information that would fall under the category of 'family secrets' and while I am not shy about letting you know this, I am somewhat reluctant to air the dirty laundry of either myself or my ancestors for others to make judgements about.

On the other hand, perhaps while I don't want to air my own dirty laundry I am not shy about airing others', since the 'family' part of family secrets really does not apply directly to me, as I still don't know who my family is. So, I have nothing to be ashamed of and nothing to dread, other than the scorn and ridicule of any current relatives that have no idea of the quest I am on or what I have or have not discovered thus far.

Being that as it may, and since I have already aired my opinion, there are a few things that have been discovered over the years that perhaps are best shared so that the reader can decide for himself or herself what is relevant and what is not. I am at the age where with the little amount of time I have left I can flip off the world and go about my daily routine and not really worry about what someone else thinks.

Or can I?

I do have a wife. I have two adult daughters and an adult son in law, all with good paying jobs and established lifestyles in their respective communities. I have five grandchildren, two of the adult stance, two more very close to it, and one bringing up the rear but will be there in a few short years. I have two older living 'siblings', and while not biologically related, are still important people in my life. And then we have nieces and nephews and so on and so forth and…

You get my drift.

What will they think? Will they care? Do I care what they will think?

Is it really important at this point in time that I seem to be the only one in my 'family' that has all the cards, all the pieces of the puzzle (well, almost…still working on that one) and ready to show my hand?

Why hasn't this question been raised before by others? Do we just go about our daily lives oblivious to what is going on around us, like an ostrich with blinders on, and deflect anything that comes our way or seems to be headed in our direction?

No, I think that the greater good comes into play in that old saying:

Wisdom comes from making good decisions.
Good decisions come from experience.
Experience comes from making bad decisions.

Years from now people will look back on this writing and some will wonder why I didn't dish out what I found in totality, while others will look back and wonder why I dished out anything at all.

And each one will be right.

There comes a time, perhaps many times, in a man's life when he is confronted with laying out the truth…the full and honest truth…and letting sleeping dogs lie. I have decided that the family secrets that are about to be revealed will only be the ones that directly affect me, not others in the family tree of 'Rathkey'.

Someone 'else' with that name, should he or she so desire, should be the 'one' to lay claim to opening up the closed wounds of the past and bare them naked to the eyes of the future. The only problem with that is that the eyes of the future are going to be looking at their information through the lens of the future, not the past.

I am trying my level best to look at the events of the past...over 70 years ago...through the lens of that period in time. I am trying my level best to understand the dynamics of what happened....the truth...but keep it in perspective and not sensationalize it beyond that which it is.

I absolutely abhor people that decry past sins of our forefathers by looking at their actions through the rosy tinted lens of the present. This serves no purpose. This serves no higher master. This only serves to incite, or ridicule, or enslave people to a way of thinking that is not germane to either the past nor the present, and certainly not the future.

I studied the past. And I shared those studies with my students and family members.

I keep in tune with the present. And I share those thoughts with my students and family members, when appropriate.

I try to keep abreast of the possible future. And I carefully prognosticate with those that understand we are looking at something not yet of our being, but that could be at our doorstep if we don't keep our eye on the ball, so to speak.

But those three scenarios...past/present/future...all have their place. Just not in the same place at the same time. And certainly not through the same lens.

So as I look back at the secrets I have learned about my since deceased paternal Grandfather Rathkey, about my since deceased 'legal' father and my mother Rathkey, about my since deceased and some still alive siblings and other relatives and friends, I find myself cautioning myself as to the 'good' that is served by exposing those secrets to the universe.

So what, that I know them and others don't?

So what, if I take them to my grave?

So what?

Lincoln once stated: 'it is sometimes better to be silent and be thought a fool than to speak and remove all doubt.'

I agree.

But that does not stop me from what I still must do.

We still need to know the following:

Who knew What?

When did they know it?

Where was it known?

How was it accomplished?

Why was it covered up?

The game is still afoot, Dr. Watson.

Sherlock says 'Ahead'.

16

HIGH SCHOOL REFLECTIONS

Waseca, Minnesota
1965-1971

Back in the day, when I was in junior high and high school, I was a really mixed up kid with multiple personalities. Or rather, a normal kid acting out normally with really weird tastes and ambitions and directions. Who knows at that age what we really 'are', with hormones jumping around, trying to find an identity to hang with that seems to be what we are but really, may just be a 'mask' as to the real inner self.

This is the conundrum that I faced starting junior high school. I was eager to be in school…not because I was a stellar student but because it gave me more opportunity to….to…I don't know, but to…

My older sister, Pauline, was off to the University of Minnesota, so there was one less person to pester me at home. But she is very smart and focused and a 'student' at heart…could be all of her life. My older brother was off to the great southwest working with VISTA (Volunteers in Service to America) after graduating from the University of Chicago with a JD degree in law. Terry was very intelligent and with a big heart…the 'caring' and tender one of my siblings. And my oldest brother, already married, was off to the great northwest working for Batelle Industries in some computer/ science/ nerd role that was beyond my realm of thinking. Bob was smart, brilliant, and forward thinking…a real dreamer.

So, it was just me and mom and dad at home on North State Street. Dad had sold his business, The Waseca Sports Shop…'the best in sporting equipment for the best in sports'…back in 1960, since neither of my older brothers had any interest in coming back and running it after graduation from college. But he was still an on shift, alternate day fireman for the City and worked on his off days either with the City Street Maintenance crew or for Lester Moat hauling company (dirt, rocks, fill, etc.) or perhaps for Merv Tau with his local carthage company. Merv would later go on to start up Lau's Meat Market on the north end of town and provide us locals with great meat cuts along with a variety of sausages and other niceties.

He also had a meat grinder that could pulverize a bull in about 60 seconds and makes the wood chipper incident in 'Fargo' look docile in comparison. He and I will have a chat about that later on, along with his son, but that is a story for another chapter.

But as I begin life as a junior high student, I am realizing that I am acting differently from grade school and being treated differently than grade school. Though my name has always been "Donny", only the girls call me that. I am called 'Butch', the same nickname as my father and older brother. Even the teachers call me by my nickname so I just roll with it.

But life in general for this first year at the high school was trying, at best. It seemed like the talents I had were not always in the normal range of what was acceptable behavior…my fingers were light, my speed fast, and my lies and profane gestures not always welcome or warranted.

I noticed that there seemed to be a correlation between my negative behaviors and punishment or discipline at home…and that was more reoccurring than not. I seemed to challenge myself to acting out and being noticed for my negative behaviors, then accepting the results of those negative actions. And then going about and doing it all over again...like an elixir that could not quench my thirst.

Wearing red pants to school was not the highlight of the year, and trying to change my mother's mind about it only made things worse at home. I seemed to be caught in a web of hand-me-downs that were not of my older brother's vintage...they were of my sisters. I was even wearing old army pants that my dad brought home from serving in WW II that mom hemmed so the inseam and waist was correct, but the end result was a 'baggy' type of garment that made me stick out like a really sore thumb.

Nice clothes for school was never really an issue, so I just had to deal with the teasing and ribbing as best I could and ignore it, until it got the best of me and I acted out in a usually negative way that would piss off someone...usually an upper classman...and then that would lead to other negative consequences.

Never mind that my grades were average, that my musical abilities were excellent, and my physical skills made others sit up and take notice. Those things don't count when the scales of school justice tip in the other direction. Lip service from 'friends' and tolerable behaviors from faculty only led to more outbursts of negative behavior.

But I soon learned that though I was the last 'Rathkey', that name still carried some weight from my older siblings and my parents...as if that was going to help me now. There seemed to be this 'aura' at home of an image that I needed to straighten up, fly right, and live up to or else...oh, here goes the threat about the Sheriff's Boys Ranch in Red Wing again. I seemed to be existing in a world that others thought I belonged to, but really didn't feel like a 'part' of it as much as an outsider looking 'in' on it.

Similar behaviors continued to plague, or surround, me as I went into 8th grade, and then into 9th.

But then something happened. Donny started to grow…grow up and out. And moreso, Donny was being recognized for talents and abilities that had been hidden or at least less productive in the past. Third week of Senior High Band (which was a really great band, by the way) and I was sitting 1st chair tuba, having beat out three other seniors in the process. And that was a seat I would not relinquish until graduation in 1971, after having achieved All State Honors for the 2nd year in a row. My parents were proud, and pleased…but things in general still hadn't changed at home.

With a solid instrumental background, coupled with my last few years of piano instruction at the hands of some very tolerant nuns over at the Sacred Heart Conservatory, my musical talents were starting to make people take notice. My final recital piece a year later would be Chopin's Polonaise in g minor…a gruelling and fast paced challenge that was memorized to the nth degree. My vocal range was also deepening, placing me in the select section of the high school choir that would later on earn me All State Honors as a senior. Again, my parents were proud, and pleased…but things in general still hadn't changed at home.

I soon began to realize that there was a direct correlation between my success in high school and the way I was treated at home. I would caustically say that I believed my mother to give or show 'love' conditionally…it was not automatically 'given' or showered upon me. I had to earn it and if I did things that were not acceptable, well, you can already guess the resulting behaviors I would suffer. Dad was more of the quiet type, and with him being 'gone' every other day due to his work schedule, he was not aware of the multitude of times that my mother and I would go round and round verbally over something that I guess I did wrong.

At least the threats of the Sheriff's Boys Ranch in Red Wing had stopped. So did the spankings, right after Dad tried to swat me with the yardstick for talking back to him and having it break against the back of my right calf. He looked at the two pieces, I looked at the two pieces, we both looked at each other, and he said 'guess that won't work anymore' and we left things at that.

But there was one incident, which will be discussed in detail in an upcoming chapter, that would cause me to react in such a manner that not only did it make me wonder if I was in the right family, but if I was indeed human with normal thoughts and normal reactions and normal mental stability. That incident would shake me to the bone and stay hidden for decades...but needs to come out in a feeling of total cleansing in order for things to be made right.

My athletic prowess and my seemingly attraction to the opposite sex seemed to kick in around my sophomore year. Earning All Conference honors in football as a placekicker and middle linebacker lead to a different perception of me in the fall of 1968. Though I was only 5'10" and 150 pounds, I could hold my own and put kickoffs into the endzone, something that was going to gain me some noteworthy attention as years would come along.

My grades started to take shape as a result of more focus on my part and showing more of an interest in the subject matter. I also was 'noticed' more by the opposite sex and while I didn't claim a 'girlfriend' at the time, I got plenty of smiles and hints as the year would unwind that it kept me on my toes with eyes open, pants zipped, and lips plumped! But all the while I am still looking at clues and behaviors that indicate something is 'wrong' or at least not right in general...but I can't put my finger on anything special or nail down anything definitive.

Winter season saw me named All Conference in wrestling as a 155 pounder. I was not the most flashy, nor the strongest, nor the most prolific wrestler on the team. But I was able to anticipate better than anyone...I paid attention to my opponents and I knew what was going to be attempted before the actual motion began, allowing me to react defensively as quickly as possible for a maneuver to counter whatever you were trying to throw at me. And I was tough as nails…I didn't care if you put me at 155 or elevated me to 165 or 175…I was going to meet you on the mat, toe to toe, and I was going to give you my best because that was what was expected of me. I owed that to my teammates, my coaches, my family and fans…and to myself.

And while there were times I got beaten, I got beaten by a better wrestler. There was no shame in that. But you were going to have to earn it…I was not going to give it to you.

Spring came around and while track was fun throwing the shot and discuss and running the low hurdles, tennis was more of a workout for me and I seemed to excel at the sport, having played it since elementary school days. I again earned All Conference honors, only being beaten once in 15 matches, and looked forward to working at Bird's Eye during the summer months earning some money for college.

But, again…was I missing 'clues' that in the future I would kick myself for due to missing them? I was still just a kid, though I was now a one-year-older kid and should be acting more like a 'Rathkey', just as my older siblings did.

Heck, there were so many things that I did not do during my high school years that my older brothers got to do on a regular basis that it drove me nuts when I finally realized that I was indeed being treated differently. I did not go duck hunting before school in a slough 5 miles from town. I did not drive solo at all during high school unless it was with Dad and the lawnmowers going out to the 3 acres to clean things up. And heck, we had a '50 Buick that was built like a Sherman tank that would part any oncoming traffic like Moses parted the Red Sea if they saw us coming…on either side of the road! Nope…nothing 'challenging' or 'dangerous' or even cautiously, possibly caustic would happen to the 'baby of the family'. Not on her watch.

But then it dawned on me…was it 'me' that was being treated differently because I was acting differently, or was it 'me' that was being treated differently because someone else was acting differently?

The term 'helicopter' parents may have originated with my parents back in the 60's and the rest of the world jumped on the verbal bandwagon and took it over. But that is exactly what was happening…my mother was hanging on to me like the last bite of apple pie because I was the 'last' of the Rathkey kids…the last visage of her motherhood and identity in the Waseca school system…and I was nearing the end of it within a few short years and that could mean the end of…..?

The end of….what?

Was she trying to protect me all of these years because she was afraid of losing her identity when the last of us…me…left home and went on to…whatever we went on to? Didn't she realize that by hovering over me and shadowing me and not allowing me to grow and grow up and make mistakes and suffer consequences that she was going to be hurting me as I did grow up and have to face challenges and consequences outside of her reach? And by then, the consequences would be hitting me harder because I had not learned those lessons earlier in life?

Well, enough of Freud as my junior and senior years were here. Now I was starting to be recognized as a "BMOC'…Big Man on Campus…and it felt good, as long as I didn't let it go to my head. Grades were good, almost too good, as my preferences were starting to show, and with all due respect to my teachers and girlfriends, I really was leaning toward a career in Biology, as it was one of my top subjects. My musical talents were awesome, almost college level talent, and my All Conference honors in football, wrestling, and tennis were right up there for recognition second only to the success I was having being a three spring sport letter winner in baseball, track, and tennis. My nickname in baseball was not 'Butch' but 'Hoover' due to my scooping ability as nothing got by me, either when playing 1st base or catching behind the plate. Though one needs to remember that I am ambidextrous…I can do things equally well with either hand, though I tend to rely more on my left for power and my right for accuracy. As a left handed catcher I threw out more runners at 1st base than those actually trying to steal 2nd…all I had to do was pivot and throw, and with a right handed batter in the box, you were mine! My bat towered home runs with power and my speed on the basepath allowed me to score from 1st on a routine single up the gap in most instances. Now about 5'11" and 165 pounds, I was a terror on the field, a demon on the mat, and one you could not catch in the hurdles.

And I still had a year to go to try and put it all together.

But still those little devils that sit on my shoulders would pop up every once in a while and challenge my sanity and my thought processes so that I would do something stupid, say something inappropriate, act out in a selfish manner, or just be a jerk for no reason at all. Summer came and I was again working at Bird's Eye, due to the efforts of my father and a good family and fellow fire fighter, Jon Hall. He kept me on the straight and narrow at work and though he has since left this realm, I thank him for his efforts and what he tried to do not only with me, but for me. He and his wife, Maria, a co-worker of Dad's in the old fire station on South State Street, are great, salt of the earth people. Much love and affection to people I still think of daily.

Well, nothing 'Rathkey' about any of those negative behaviors, at least according to my parents. Better keep your nose to the grindstone, focused, and let everything else and everyone else that is 'irrelevant' slip to the cheap seats and watch from the side. We still have another year with you at home and we all need to get through it.

As Ramses said in 'The Ten Commandments'…'so let it be written, so let it be done'.

But I also learned during the summer that, while working across the street from the home of a 'new' girlfriend, unless you paid attention, and I mean attention, to her on a daily basis, let alone a weekly one, things were not going to go well. And when things don't go well, well, Donny tends to act out in a negative way that is not productive to anyone or anything around him. Again, nothing 'Rathkcy' about those behaviors!

Senior year rolled around in the fall of 1970 and All Conference accolades in football, wrestling, track, baseball, and tennis, along with All State status for both band and choir, were routine and didn't hold the same 'honor' as it did before. At least not for me. Heck, my parents were proud as punch, because of the status that it gave them. Almost like a redemption for the things I had done in the past that they had suffered for.

Back in the day, I held the school, conference, and state records for the longest field goal in an athletic competition at 53 yards. My wrestling skills earned me scholarships from regional colleges and universities. My senior year in tennis I was undefeated until mono hit me right before tournament time, and I was 17 and 0 and held, and still do, the state record for being the only high school heavyweight to earn All Conference honors and go undefeated in tennis in the same year, a record that still stands. Post high school baseball offers came in, and I was inundated with offers from major universities to be in their marching and concert bands and select choirs.

But still...things were not the same.

And it was not that I was getting bored, but I was just getting...bored and unchallenged. I knew that once graduated, and off to the University (it was already planned that the U of Minnesota was going to be my landing place, not so much for my physical talents as much as my parents limited financial resources and with the U being a land grant college, well...the 'Rathkey' tradition at the U of M would continue, come hell or high water).

Always wanted to go to Purdue, but, well…reality is what it is.

But there was still an incident from my freshman year that was haunting me, and would continue to haunt me for years and years to come, until I decided to take things into my own hands and deal with it once and for all.

Sometimes, you just have to say 'enough is enough' and stand up, take either your lumps or dish them out, and consequences be damned. I tried to bury that incident for years, only to have it come back and taunt me, and it didn't seem to matter in what arena I was being challenged, that taunt was always there. And it was affecting how I dealt with people, how I treated people, and how I looked upon myself.

The only question that remained, at this point in time, was… when? When do I confront it and in what manner do I want to deal with it?

Permanently!

17

PIECING THE PUZZLE TOGETHER

Crystal and Waseca, Minnesota
March and April, 2025

Our 30th President, Calvin Coolidge, once said:

> Nothing in the world can take the place of persistence. Talent will not; nothing is more common than unsuccessful men with talent. Genius will not; unrewarded genius is almost a proverb. Education will not; the world is full of educated derelicts. Persistence and determination alone are omnipotent. The slogan 'Press on!' has solved and always will solve the problems of the human race.

I liked that, and if I was anything, it was like a bloodhound on the trail of a bone when it came to solving this puzzle of not only who I was but where I came from, my ancestry, and when did people know things.

And I guess I was beginning to wonder…why keep me in the dark all these years?

Well, certain pieces of the puzzle were on the board, but there were gaps and missing pieces that needed to be accounted for in order for this thing to not only take shape but also to make sense. And it seemed to me that since I had exhausted, or at least thought I had exhausted, the family and background material that I had on hand in our home in Crystal, the answers must lie in Waseca, and whatever or whomever was still around and alive that could help shed light on this nightmare.

So…these last few months it was necessary for me to go to Waseca, under the guise of getting future hunting sites in order and to check on older relatives, hence, the trip needed to be done by me on a solo mission and not include my wife, Julie. She seemed readily to accept my reasoning, since she has not met most of these people and to spend the greater part of the day tramping around in some woods or field edges looking for deer sign was just not appealing. So things worked out all the way around.

As I was driving down 35W on my one of many trips south to Waseca it suddenly dawned on me that there were probably other files of Dr. Hampton that I had not searched in my initial inquiries, so my first stop had to be the medical historical section of the Court House Annex, the old Ben Franklin store.

I saw Barb again at the front desk, indicated to her what I needed to find and for her to point me in the closest right direction so I could ascertain the files I was looking for. She gave me a slight grin and raised eyebrow, then directed me to the historical archives that housed medical records and notes from previous decades, way back to the early 1900's.

As I made my way back along the stacks I did not notice her immediately grab her cell phone and make a quick, but quiet phone call.

I found the stacks I was looking for, and my search of previous files would be redundant to try and research again, so I delved more into the hospital system files of who was where and when on the date of my birth, hoping that I might find a shred of evidence that would indicate some more pieces of my puzzle were beginning to take shape.

And take shape they were. I looked at the personnel records and early October shift assignments, and suddenly one more piece of the puzzle seemed to jump out at me. I had to remember that the early morning hours of October 6th was home to a terrific rain and wind storm in Waseca, and things were topsy turvy for several hours and days thereafter, so some things may seem off kilter compared to what was supposed to be present. I kept that in mind and pressed on.

With this new piece of information fully vetted I now had to search other files for the dispensation of patients as they were admitted and discharged from the hospital. Going through those files was tedious and time consuming, but Dr. Hampton left very complete anecdotal notes and records in his lifetime, and the ones I found relative to October 6, 1953 and the weeks thereafter were priceless.

Is it possible she was still alive?

Is it possible, if she still lives, that she would remember and be able to shed light and fill in the gaps as to what really happened that morning?

Only one way to find out.

At least now some more of the pieces of the puzzle were beginning to come together, but there were still gaps as to the 'actual' order of events and who was involved in the deceptions surrounding my birth.

Several hours later, as I was going to leave the Annex for what seemed like an eternity of studying files and notes, as I was saying 'goodbye' to Barb at the front desk, she handed me a note and smiled.

The note, addressed to 'Donny', simply asked me to come by for a visit at my earliest convenience…I would know the place, and any time she would be accessible. Just let the front desk know.

I was dumbfounded! I turned to Barb, only to find she was already gone and out of sight. I stopped, re-read the note and realized that I had no idea where I was to go or whom I was about to see.

'I would know the place…let the front desk know'.

'I would know…..'!

Of course!

She WAS still alive and aware of my situation.

But HOW?

I wasted no time and drove over to Lakeshore Inn Nursing Home, the residence of my mother for the last few years of her life and a place that I knew very well. When I was smaller my folks… well, Leon and Irma, would often take me there on Sunday afternoons as they/we visited with elderly residents and relatives, since it was the only nursing home in the area worth a damn. I usually wandered around while mom and dad talked with their friends, and reunited with them sometime later after exploring on my own.

While the layout had changed somewhat over the years since I was last there when my mom passed away back in 1998, the same general aura of the place was the same and I knew when I got there exactly whom I was to seek. That part of the Annex files was starting to come back to me and pieces of the puzzle were now floating around in my head, not quite in place but close enough for some gaps to become smaller.

Going to her room, I was shocked to see a crew from the funeral home escorting out a body already encased in a plastic body bag with a religious ceremonial cloth over the transport. I stood at attention while they passed, still in a state of shock, when I was confronted by a kindly, older residential staffing nurse who directed me back to the room from which the body had just been removed.

She went to a dresser top, pulled out an old, dusty envelope with my name on it and instructed me that Floris Splitter wanted me to have this, in the event we were not able to talk in person.

But I was just given a note to see her not more than a few hours ago, and the note directed me to come and visit her at any time at this place. How could she not be here when I arrived? How could she have left me in the lurch and darkness of this nightmare just when I needed her the most?

I was told that Floris Splitter, Doris's twin sister, was in poor and failing health for quite some time, but seemed to be holding on as if she was waiting for someone to come and see her. She had the strength and internal fortitude of an ox, but the will to live was simply overcome by the cancerous invasion of her bodies entire organ system. This was simply her time to go, and even though she waited with anticipation of the arrival of 'someone', she didn't have the strength to carry on anymore.

But she did have help in those final days…help that I did not ascertain until it was too late. But once I figured out what was going on, I was thankful for the brief time I was able to spend with her in the Annex and the help she gave Floris in her final days.

You see, Barb at the Court House Annex was Floris's niece, and Doris's adopted daughter. Doris left us many years prior, seemingly oblivious to some things going on around her from her medical past, but Floris had stayed sharp and when informed by her niece that I was in town several months ago, and what I was searching for, Floris figured it was only a matter of time before I put 2 and 2 together and came a calling, if I knew where to call.

Hence, the letter. A proactive approach that she hoped she would not need but in the end was the lynchpin that helped put part of the puzzle together.

But the confusing part of the letter was not what was written in black in white, dictated to Barb with her actually writing the letter in Floris's own words, but the very old, bent skeleton key that was included with the letter. That part puzzled me beyond comprehension, along with the void of 'no discernible words' indicating what it was or where it came from, other than the word 'twin' which was included in the letter in the form of an identification tag and attached by old twine to the key.

As I was leaving, Barb was entering the building and was in tears, so we sat down and visited in the lobby area that over looked Loon Lake. She had just been informed of her Aunt's passing when I had entered the building and I was so glad to have seen her again before I left.

We visited for awhile, with Barb 'wondering' if I had gotten all that I came for? I told her I had missed visiting with her Aunt by just moments but that I had the letter left for me and that I would read it later, along with trying to figure out the 'key' situation.

Barb really had no idea of the key and its' significance, so she was of no help to me there. But she did indicate that if I had any other questions, to give her a call or stop by either the Annex or her home to visit about the situation I found myself in. She was most empathetic and while she could not give me all that I was looking for, she certainly knew that this weighed heavily on my mind and that I needed to get to the bottom of it as soon as I possibly could.

Analysis of the letter later on would reveal a rather cryptic message, one that asked me to remember that late night in April of 1998 when my mother passed away.

'Remember your last moments. Trace your steps from the nursing home driveway back to Irma's room. Remember who was there and who was not and who was leaving. Think back to your last words to your mother, and your actions, and most importantly, remember her last words to you. That is the key you need to remember...her last words to you.'

I went back outside to the nursing home driveway, sat in my truck, and racked my brain thinking back to that late evening. I do remember my last moments from the driveway to her room. I do remember who was there, I remember who was leaving her room, and who was stepping out for a few minutes to take a break.

I remember well my last words to my mother, her failing grip on my hand with her still ever-sharp nails, what she pressed in my hand, and her whispered last words to me…

Her whispered last words to me…her whis…

Oh, my God!

Now it was all coming back, as clear as newly frozen ice on a glacial lake.

Now it was all starting to make sense. But I still did not have all of the pieces that I needed to put this puzzle, and my past life, to rest. I needed more.

And in order to do that, I needed to get back to Crystal and the one thing my grandfather Hans left for me that may solve this entire riddle.

The pieces were mostly there, but not all of them. There were still gaps and no observant methods of making sense of the many pieces and fragments.

There still had to be an explanation that would tie them all together.

Bits and pieces and old notes and letters and a key with a cryptic message were only teasing me as to the final disposition. That I would have to find on my own.

But then what?

Indeed…..then what?

18

MORE REFLECTIONS

Crystal, Minnesota
May, 2025

Whenever I go downstairs to my 'man cave' office area, and sit in my old leather recliner with soft music on in the background, I find myself in a perfect setting for looking back in time to places and times long since gone from my immediate field of everyday radar activities.

Since this quest of a nightmare started over a year ago, I find myself retreating more and more to my recliner, drifting off and remembering those things from the past that were good, those that were terrible, and those that were neither...they were just there and happened in the course of a day.

My college days as an undergrad the University of Minnesota were some of the best, and worst, times in my life. Had I known then what I am trying to understand now, I would have done things differently.

But while success has many fathers, failure is usually an orphan. Somebody famous once said that...don't know who, don't know when. Just know...

But of the several successes that I did have in college, one stands out that until now, was not known to the general public; heck, not even my family knew. And my older sister, Pauline, lived just a few block away from me just off the St. Paul Campus home I called Bailey Hall, and she never found out.

Until now.

What the hell…more truths will soon be exposed, might as well start to open the can of worms now and see what crawled out!

I went to the U of M on a full academic scholarship, with a major in sociology that would give me options upon graduation. I wanted to be a high school social studies teacher and coach, but, hey…this is the '70's and people change majors like changing their underwear. But I also had something else going for me.

I was selected for the 'Pride of Gold Country'…the U of M Marching Band, a band my oldest brother, Bob had been in for 4 years back in the late 50's as an undergrad and one that I looked forward to joining. My musical abilities were generous and it was easy being part of something greater than yourself.

But being on the football field with my baritone was not as fulfilling to me as being on the football field in another uniform… that of the Golden Gopher Football Team.

As a high school athlete, and way before that, my Dad would usually take me to one football game each season, usually a late, winter cold, snow filled game against a late season opponent like Iowa or Wisconsin. It was great, and warm or cold, just being out with dad in that 60,000+ Memorial Stadium with his pipe or cigar smoke swirling around both our heads, man, it just don't get any better than that.

At least, not when you are a small boy with wonder in his eyes, looking at those behemoths running around the football field knocking the hell out of each other!

Well, to keep this part of the story rolling, my athletic skills allowed me to practice on my own on the baseball/softball field behind Bailey Hall on the St. Paul Campus. I had an old football and tee and when the urge hit me, usually every other day, I would go out on the practice field and kick the ball around just to stay in shape and pretend that there were goal posts the ball was sailing through from 60 yards or further!

Well, it seems my skills became known to another University professor, Mr. Tom Coucher, a former Gopher himself on the basketball court, former coach of the professional Minneapolis Laker basketball team (forerunner to the Los Angeles Lakers) and former head coach of the Golden Gopher men's basketball team, now a physical education professor relegated to the St. Paul Campus in his 'golden years' or pre-retirement years, as kind words would state.

Mr. Coucher had been watching me and since I was also one of his intramural sports officials in my 'spare' time (ya, right....spare time in college???) he called me in one afternoon, got in touch with a former equipment manager on the Minneapolis campus, and got me a regulation college football and tee and told me the Gophers would like for me to try out as a 'walk-on' (non recruited and non scholarship) player as soon as I was available.

Damn...this could not be getting any better! Paulie Terlog was the football coach and putting on the maroon and gold, only this time in another uniform, was a great goal of mine. I still have those pictures on my downstairs picture board, taken on Press Day with me, in uniform, with my ball and tee and Memorial Stadium in the background. And the final picture standing between mom and dad after the annual spring game, holding my helmet and smiling because I had kicked the only two extra points of my college career during that game...and on a bad knee.

But why I was wearing number '17', white jersey, in practice, but wearing number '96', maroon jersey, for the game is another story and perhaps another book in the wings!

But I digress....that part of the chapter is for another story sometime else, not here.

To make a long story shorter, Paulie Terlog was fired and Hal Moeller from Wake Forest was stepping in as the new head coach. A former Gopher lineman himself back in the Bernie Biermann hay-days of national football prominence for the U of M was one of the reasons he was chosen…take us back to the 'good old days' with that veer offense, torrid ground game, and limited passing attack, kinda like Oklahoma.

Well, winter conditioning was grueling and I went from a 6', 175 pound college freshman to a 6'1", 225 pound aggressive, in your face monster in a little over 3 months. This allowed me to end up as the 2nd team kicker behind Stew Flair, an upperclassman from Canada and a 3rd string middle linebacker behind two players that would later get drafted and play in the NFL for the Baltimore Colts and St. Louis Cardinals.

Remember, this is back in the early '70's…get the names right!

Unfortunately, a left knee injury took me out of the equation in pretty short order just a week before the annual spring game, and while not opting for surgery at the time, that knee would never be the same. Getting knee surgery in the early '70's was a deal breaker and career ender, so, let's move on.

Having a recruited placekicker and punter come in from Wyandotte, Michigan, Tank Lotso, did little for my ego and I saw the writing on the wall. I did go on to captain the Gopher rugby team a year later and earn All Conference 1st team honors, and we won the Big Ten Tournament that spring at the University of Illinois down in Champagne, Illinois…highlites of that year. Still gimpy on my knee but able to get around, I focused on my classes and my upcoming sophomore year at the U.

Well…that was the 'story' that most people knew of, believed, and lived by.

But there were some nefarious things going on at the U during that time period, and by luck of the draw or just plain being in the right place at the right time, my 'walk on' experience on the football team...

... was all a hoax!

I was a 'plant'. That meeting with Mr. Coucher was also a recruiting meeting with a representative of the Minneapolis branch of the F.B.I...Federal Bureau of Investigations.

Holy crap on a cracker! What the hell have I just stumbled upon?

Turns out, again, to make a long story short...the FBI was concerned about a drug problem infiltrating the athletic department and worried that illicit, pain reducing drugs and other types of illegal drugs might become prevalent on the campus and it was ordered to put a stop to it as soon as possible.

But FBI agents don't look like college students, so they hire students to go undercover (yup...got paid $500 and a new set of clothes) and get information so they can make a bust later on when the evidence piles up enough for a warrant to be issued.

Seems like Mr. Coucher had done the same thing as an undergrad when he was at the U, and his contacts with them still remained strong, so he recommended they take a look at me and if things worked out, I would go 'in' and see what I could uncover.

Turns out 1/3 of all regular FBI agents have a law background; 1/3 have a law enforcement background; and 1/3 of them have a sociology background, due to the amount of time we spend studying human behavior.

That was me! And this was were my IQ testing score of 163 was validated...by the frickin' FBI!

Talk about de ja vue, all over again!

I can't go into specifics, as I am still under a NDA (non disclosure agreement) while I am still in my '70's, but suffice to say things were discovered, information shared, warrants drawn up and executed, people apprehended, and a few roster changes made from 1971 to 1972 in several sports on the U of M campus.

My knee injury was 'real', though, and almost blew the entire operation wide open. But luckily, for them and for me, it brought people to my doorstep with exactly the merchandise the FBI was looking for, so the sting worked and I stayed hurt.

Damn! That was not supposed to be part of the equation!

As far as I know, no one in my immediate family knew or got wind of any of this, and will only know about it if reading this book. Sorry, sister Pauline…had to keep things on the down low due to the NDA, but now that you know….so what? 😊

Suffice to say I was proud to wear the maroon and gold in three different U of M arenas:

1. Academic (honor student, Dean's list, and Presidential Scholar, in addition to adding two graduate degrees, Specialist in Secondary Administration and a PhD in Educational Administration, along with post-doctoral work in educational administration on a $50,000 BUSH Foundation scholarship at Harvard, Dartmouth, and the University of San Francisco);
2. Athletic (Golden Gopher football team and rugby Team as Captain and Most Valuable Player, along with representing the U at various athletic functions); and the
3. Arts (Marching Band for two years, being selected as a Rank Lieutenant for my sophomore year, only the 3rd such honor given in the entire history of the marching band to an underclassman, as Rank Lieutenants are almost exclusively seniors and possibly a few juniors).

These honors led to my induction into the U of M '3A' Hall of Fame back in 2007, an honor I was humble to accept, and with gratitude and pride still cherish.

But again, if I knew then what I know now, would things have been different? I don't know. I only know that my behaviors started to settle down, well, except for a few instances when the devil in me just decided to have his way and the heck with whatever anyone else was thinking or saying. Those repercussions could have been disastrous and deeply affect my career, in all areas of development.

But as I look back, except for one very dark cloud that still was hanging over my head for whatever reason, things started to just settle down and be on course for a productive career, both professionally and personally.

But that cloud was still there, and it seemed to be growing based on what I was hearing.

Does it get ignored, or do I have to stand up to it and face it someday, once and for all?

Either way, my life will be changed, and not necessarily for the better, for sometimes you need a certain level of mutual self destruction, along with the object of focus, in order for justice to be done.

Sounds self deprecating, and lethal, but…

You don't always get to have your cake and eat it, too.

But what I have been hearing, coupled with what I experienced years ago on that Central High School playground, makes me realize that dormant feelings of the dark side are beginning to stir, and beginning to rise to the surface of my mental capacities. What had been buried for years is beginning to smolder and simmer and bring about deep feelings of hatred and revenge and in a weird sense…justicc…for those unable to fend for themselves.

The law enforcement background memories of my grandfather and father are on one shoulder, balancing the dark side feelings from gaining majority control of my actions that are wavering on the other shoulder, tetering periously close to a full tilt.

That man done messed with the wrong hombre years ago. But this time it will not start or end with a sucker punch.

But that showdown is still on the horizon, hopefully years away, if ever.

Like my 'alternate personality' that dominates when I am archery hunting, I become an assassin…sitting quietly, in the blind or in the tree, regulated breathing and eyes moving before the head turns on a swivel. Quiet, deliberate, like a fer de lance waiting to strike. And when the arrow leaves the string and the bow, death travels with it.

But the potential for a showdown is always present, always still there. Waiting.

19

SAFE SECRETS AND REVELATIONS

Crystal, Minnesota
Late May, 2025

Horace Greeley once proclaimed:

'Fame is a vapor.
Popularity is an accident.
Money takes wings.
The only thing that endures is character'.

Lord only knows what kind of character I have turned into over the past 71 years, but the past year + has been a whirlwind of a nightmare that just doesn't seem to let up and catch me a break that I can understand.

I am left with bits and pieces, this and that, speculations and theories, guesses and ideas…but what I need is solid, irrefutable proof as to my origin, my identity, and how I fit into the overall scheme of things relative to the name 'Rathkey'.

I have spent hours, alone and in deep thought, trying to visualize past events and personnel encounters so as to shed some light on the direction I may go to put this all together and, finally, behind me. But all I keep coming up with is dead ends, with possibilities but not probabilities. That is not good enough. But I must persist.

I took time to sit down at my man cave desk in the basement and assemble all of the pieces of the puzzle that I had garnered thus far. There were old historical records, there were old medical records, there were old anecdotal records, there were pictures, there was the DNA testing samples that I had sent to Desiree out in Oregon, there was the letter from Floris, with the key…and there were memories. Vivid, but cloudy.

But there was a piece missing.

I am thinking back to my most recent information, the letter from Floris. She wanted me to go back to 1998 and remember my last few moments with my mother on the night she died at Lake Shore Inn Nursing Home. She wanted me to remember the last words that my mother spoke to me, and she wanted me to remember what my mother pressed into my hand just before she passed, again, saying in a whisper, those same words over and over and over.

'My victory's safe'…'my victory's safe'…'my victory's safe'.

'Yes, mother', I replied, 'your victory is safe. Feel free to let go, and look for Dad'.

'My victory is safe'.

'Yes, mom…go in peace. Look for Dad'.

Those were the final words my mother heard from me, and the final words that my mother spoke to me, several times, before she passed away. She had pressed her hand into mine, released the object, and slowly slipped away.

A key.

An old, bent skeleton key.

A key that I had no idea what it was for, or where to use it, so I quickly put it into my pocket as my sister came into the room, to be met with the news of our mother's passing. And I basically forgot about the key for several days.

Upon going back home to Grove City, I put the key on the top of the old secretary that was in our hallway, an antique from the days of my grandfather and grandmother Rathkey that they used to have in their home but was relegated to the basement of our 'new' home on North State Street in Waseca upon the passing of those older folks and the building of our new home. It was too nice of a piece of furniture to be let go or stay in storage, so my wife, Julie, graciously accepted it as a family heirloom and we found a place, somewhat out of the way but still visible, for other family pictures, bibles, and records of the Rathkey ancestry. The key lay on its' side next to the gold watch of my maternal grandfather, Warren Scarton, for years and years...didn't know where it went...didn't care.

But now, almost 30 years later, I am confronted with the fact that the key my mother pressed into my hand and the key that was in the letter Floris Splitter left for me were identical to each other...twins!

Two keys for the same lock, and no idea where that lock was located.

Now I am really frustrated, as pieces of the puzzle seem to be floating around in space and not coming together to help me solve this dilemma. I don't need more pieces of the puzzle disjointed and not congruent with each other...I need things to come together.

But then I decided to relax in my recliner and just think... free thinking without any guardrails to keep me focused. Just free thoughts of what people had said and what evidence I had in front of me that could fit together and make sense of this quagmire.

It came to me that while I had one key given to me from my mother back in 1998 at the very night of her passing, and another identical key given to me on the very night of the passing in 2025 of a family friend and confidant, there had to be a connection. There just had to be! There had to be some joining of these two events and objects, all directed at me, that would help me bring closure to this decade of question.

But what was it?

The really odd thing about those keys, after hours and hours of reflection, was the fact that both keys were slightly bent in the middle, as if someone had taken it and bent it using a vise or hammered it bent using a ball pean hammer. It made no sense…a 2" bent key, with a 15 degree bend in it.

What in sam hill could that open?

That was enough mental strain for the evening and I retired to bed way ahead of Julie, my nightowl. Sometimes my head is so swimming with thoughts and ideas that it just can't shut down and I will lay awake for hours and hours just thinking. Resting, horizontally, but not sleeping and certainly not in REM mode like most people need for a good nights' sleep.

Nope…just laying there…

And then it hit me like a ton of bricks!

I had seen that bent key before…but where? My memory banks were in overdrive and I had to pinpoint not only when but where I had seen that same distinct key.

On a hunch, but a calculated one, I got up, got dressed, scared the hell out of my wife and opened the side door to our home to a slight breeze on a moonlit night and promptly went to the garage.

There, in the back northeast corner of our Crystal garage, sat an old safe that decades before was used by my grandfather Rathkey in his places of business in Waseca. That safe would then go to my father to be used in his old Coast to Coast store on State Street in downtown Waseca, and then move across the street east to the Waseca Sports Shop, the last business my father owned but sold in 1960. That safe would then find its' way downstairs to our basement in our home on North State Street and stay there until my father's passing in 1996, whereupon it came into my possession.

Now, this 400# safe was nothing short of a monster to move and lift. I know, because back in the day I was the one that was doing the lifting. I could hold my own 30 years ago…the last time I had to physically move it by myself, but a hunk of metal that weighed that much was nothing to trifle with.

But it was mine to trifle with! I can remember years ago my father saying that his father, my grandfather, always wanted me to have that safe when the time came for me to have it. And my father always told my other siblings that when the time came for property disbursements, the safe was to go to me.

That made me feel special. Don't know why, but it did. And I remember Dad opening the safe once…only once…in the basement of our Waseca home just to give me a peek as to what the inside looked like. No papers or money or valuables there. In fact, it was bare as a baby's butt in winter, so I was not really impressed other than the fact that it was going to be mine.

I remember the slip of paper that Dad gave me with the written combination on it, in his handwriting: 14, 4 times to the right; 36, 2 times to the left; 63, 1 time to the right, then turn it back until it hits 27. Twist the handle and presto chango…your lock will open.

Ya, well after Dad's passing and me lugging that damn safe back to our Grove City home I tried the safe, several times, and could not get the damn thing to open. I began to think that weather and age and just plain rusting of old parts and gears had something to do with it, but it was an antique from my grandfather, then my father, and now was mine to do with as I pleased.

And looking at it, I now realized what my mother's last words to me were:

Mom was not saying 'My victory's safe'…

She was saying 'My Victor Safe'. She was talking about the damn safe!

The safe was a Victor Patent safe from 1885, made by the Victor Safe and Lock Company out of Cincinnati, Ohio. The logo…'In Hoc Signo Vincimus'…roughly translated from Latin to English means 'in this sign, we conquer', though the sign can be a cross within a crown, or a Phoenix rising from the ashes. Like ours.

And the front of the safe, with its' black finish and gold plated paint job with a phoenix rising from an ash fire in the middle, showed a bent skeleton key just underneath the logo, 'IN HOC SIGNO VINCIMUS'.

The key belonged to the safe…but there was no outside lock for it to fit into!

The safe opened only by combination on the outside, with no place for a key whatsoever. That meant only one thing…

The key was to be used for a locked compartment on the inside of the safe.

But now I am met with three immediate concerns:

1. Why were there two keys given to me? One by my mother and one by Floris?
2. What was the relationship between the original holders of those two keys?
3. The combination Dad gave me, in his own handwriting, does not work. How do I break into a century old safe to find 'whatever' it is inside that some old relatives obviously want me to find, but don't give me a chance to do so?

I don't want to break into a safe and damage it in the process, but at this point in time, I am at a loss not only for words but clearly thought-out plans. It is 3am and I am beginning to show not only my age but my desire for sleep. This quest will have to continue another day when I can put more stable thought into it and come up with a plan that will work.

Several days have passed since my late night venture into the garage, and my wife is starting to worry about me and what I may be up to…so Julie and I sit down and have a heart to heart. She is the smartest person I know…bookwise…and I know she will have an opinion as to not only what she would do but also what I should do.

I repeat…she will have an opinion.

But coming clean about this whole year long process and bringing her up to speed on what was going on, what I suspected, and what I surmised only helped her to guide me to think outside of the box more and come up with some other ideas that I would not normally have thought of.

I am more of a 'concrete-sequential' person, as it fits my old career profile of an educational administrator. Julie is more of an 'abstract-random' individual…totally opposite from me…yet that is what seems to help make us compatible. We each have some similar strengths, which can cause heads to sometimes get butted. But we also seem to cover each other's limitations, which in the long run, is what a partnership is supposed to do. Neither of us cares who gets the credit as long as things get done in the end.

And Julie gets the credit!!! ☺

But this one has us stymied, until Julie gives me an idea that was not thought of before…and it is brilliant!

We go back and examine the slip of paper that my father gave me years ago with his handwriting on it and the combination to the Victor floor safe. I then compare it to another slip of paper that I had tucked away in an old dresser valet that my father had given me in which there was a second combination written on it.

The two sets of handwriting did not match.

After carefully examining both pieces of paper, then digging out my grandfather's Rathkey's old German Bible from the secretary in the front hallway, I could easily see that the piece of paper given me by my father, with the combination on it, was the 'original' combination that my grandfather had written out years ago, with the piece of paper actually dated 1956…3 years after my birth and 1 month before his death.

But if that was his handwriting and the old combination, that meant that the 'new' combination that was in my father's handwriting had to be the one that opened the safe.

We could not get out to the garage fast enough in the rain to go to the safe and try the new combination…one that was not going to be hard for me to remember.

The first turn was the number 10, 4 times to the right; then the number 6, 2 times to the left; followed by the number 19, one turn to the right; and one final turn to the number 53.

My birthday: 10 6 1953. October 6th, 1953.

My immediate thoughts were Grandfather Rathkey knew something, I am just not sure what at this point in time.

This was followed by 'my father knew something', I am just not sure what at this point in time.

So…Stop and open the safe.

The combination was entered, the handle turned, and presto chango…

The damn door opened!

To a fully empty safe!

There was not a blessed thing in that safe…not a shred of paper, not a coin or paper bill, not even a scrap of old junk mail.

Nothing…just some empty cubby slots and one that needed a key to open.

Holy crap on a cracker!

A key to open…as in…a bent skeleton key that I had two copies of!

We ran back in the rain to the house, almost knocking each other over, running to the top of the secretary in the front hallway and to the valet in my dressing room so that we had both keys in our possession, just in case something nefarious was going on that we needed to be ready for.

We jogged back in the rain to the garage, bent down, and used the first key to slip in the slot and turn.

The key moved to the right and the secured door to the locked slot opened…and an old letter fell out. The letter looked like it was 100 years old as it was tainted crème in color with frayed edges and tattered and stained markings, but it clearly said on the outside of the envelope:

'To my Grandson…Donny'.

This letter was not from my Dad…it was from Grandpa Rathkey!

Holy crap on a cracker!

This old letter, which had to be written decades and decades ago, was addressed to me and was still sealed and showed no signs of being tampered with from the time it was put in the safe and sealed with the key, whenever that was, until we opened the safe now in spring, 2025.

But that was not the only surprise that was awaiting us.

The bottom of the safe was a sturdy iron/steel composite that looked like it was strong enough to hold not only money but gold bullion and other precious metals. Further research by me indicated that The Victor Safe Company was known to have floor safes that were burglar proof, water proof, and fire proof.

OK…that makes sense. But why glue a piece of old carpet to the bottom of the inside safe floor when it was plenty safe without it?

Unless…

You were trying to soften the 'blow' of something you wanted to put in there that was really valuable, or…

Unless you were trying to hide something under the carpet in the first place?

Sure enough, there was just a sliver of an edge of the carpet that came exposed after all these years and the crème-colored corner of another envelope was seen peeking out from under the carpet.

Damn…this day started out horseshit and has just gotten better and better as it goes on!

I showed Julie a better look at what I was seeing, and we agreed that there was 'something' under that carpet. What, we didn't know…but we were going to be careful and try and find out.

I carefully tugged at the exposed edge of the frayed corner of carpet and carefully peeled back the carpet, but only enough to slide what turned out to be an envelope from its' hiding place. It, like the one above it in the locked compartment, was an old gringy crème color with frayed edges and moldy smells.

It was at that point that I reached over to my workbench in the garage and had both Julie and me put on latex gloves for any further examination of the two envelopes since we didn't know when they were placed in there and what may be growing on them or had died on them over the years.

Better safe than sorry…this could be some early Ebola shit that I want nothing to do with!

We were both so giddy at this point that we decided to leave the safe open, but take the envelopes inside and put them in zip lock bags over night until we were more settled down to look at them. I still was pondering several questions relative to who, what, when, and why…but at least part of the 'where' was answered.

In my safe!

But this little excursion to the garage only deepened my quest to find out more about my situation…we had to do some more digging and we had to start putting more pieces of the puzzle together now that we had more pieces of the puzzle.

Though questions still abound about who knew what and when, there are still many 'why' questions that need to be answered, if indeed they can be.

Perhaps too much time has passed, as have the key players, so that all we have left is conjecture, in spite of or despite the pieces of 'evidence' that seem to be coming in right and left now.

But emotions, while running high, need to be kept in check as we are now at the critical stage of this quest. We have enough information to start and put the pieces together, and we need to follow the evidence and not jump to conclusions where there are gaps in sequence or in actual factual data.

But, holy crap…there has to be an ending to this soon, or I am going to go nuts.

It's one thing to 'wonder' about things form your past that you may or not be privy to when it comes to knowledge. But at least in those situations, you have a base of operations to start from and proceed.

I feel like I jumped, my parachute may or may not open, and the ground may or may not come up to meet me in a timely manner. Either way, I'm screwed.

Might as well enjoy the fall. It only hurts when you hit bottom.

And then it's all over.

For good.

20

WHO KNEW WHAT? WHEN?

Crystal, Minnesota
June, 2025

It has taken me the better part of a month to put all the pieces of this nightmare of a puzzle together, at least, all the pieces on the same sorting table. And it has taken me the better part of that month to arrange, then rearrange, then finally come to what I believe to be the best possible conclusion based on the evidence that I have in my possession.

Some of the analysis is sketchy, at best, and with most if not all of the principals already passed on, trying to think what they were thinking, or to pretend to know what was on their minds, is sometimes nothing but blatant speculation, to say the least.

But with that being said, I will now lay out for you this enigma wrapped in a conundrum, surrounded by a quagmire of information that involves not only my past, but also my present and will have a direct impact on my future.

Over the past month I had to go back in time to the late 1890's, then the 1920's and 1930's, then on to the 1950's, followed by the mid 1970's, up to the late 1990's, and finally to the past few years and now the present day in 2025.

The written evidence and clues that were left behind, some on purpose and some by sheer accident, finally found the light of day and with the help of my very intelligent and capable wife, Julie, we finally put this puzzle together so that all of the pieces fit.

Well…fit might be a stretch of the imagination, in places. But the scenario and the dialogue that accompanied such scenes was vintage genius, if not brilliant. Who would have imagined that over a hundred years could have passed before some of this written information would see the light of day?

And who, in their right mind, decades and decades ago, would have thought that key evidence still with human contact would remain for it to be found, even with the passing of those dear loved and trusted ones?

I mean…who would have thunk it?

But, again…the pieces are here. And so is the story, at least as well as I could interpret it from the evidence at hand.

If in your minds gaps still remain, either in the telling of this story or the sharing of evidence, those errors are mine and mine alone. I will not spread out any fault to anyone but myself, for those dear souls were only acting in the best interests of the loved ones and friends that entrusted them years ago with information that would soon become priceless and of such impact as to cause such present day consternation.

Buckle up, buttercup. This ride is about to get very bumpy!

First of all, let's deal with a somewhat 'minor' letter left to me from my grandfather Rathkey. I am not sure his reasoning at the time of this brief letter, but he must have known that somewhere down the line, this Victor Patent safe would end up in my possession, even though I was only 3 years old at the time of his passing.

But it was his explicit desires, as outlined in his will and last testament, that the safe belong to me 'when the time was right'… whenever that was and by whom it was to be decided that it should come into my possession.

Well, as luck or family would have it, that safe followed possession from my grandfather Rathkey to my father, Leon, from grandfather's places of business in the early to mid 1900's to those businesses of my father, from the early 1950's to the early 1960's, then to the basement of our North State Street home in Waseca. That means that any paperwork put into the safe had to occur during those time periods, and with the passing of my grandfather Rathkey in 1956, 3 years after my birth, and a subsequent safe combination change also occurring over the years, there were some pretty active people trying to either cover up, disguise, or completely subtrefuge information that would later be critical to the understanding of my existence.

Let's start with grandfather Rathkey.

The letter he left me, under lock and key (skeleton key, by the way…one of the 'twins') in the safe, told a story that he wanted me to know. Why, I have no idea, as I had two older brothers and an older sister that perhaps might have become interested in such a story, had they had any interest in following the leads and clues left behind to follow.

But, no…it was Donny and his documented IQ of 163 and an interest in history that led to the final disposition of the truth behind the safe and what happened over 100 years ago in the early days of the county of Waseca, the city of Waseca, and the State Bank of Waseca, located downtown on the corner of North State Street and 2nd Avenue.

It seems from historical files, along with my grandfather's letter, that back in the late 1890's there was a band of three brothers from the Otisco area, south of Waseca about 7 miles, that were nefarious in their motives and downright cutthroat in their dealings with people. Such was known to my grandfather Rathkey for at the time, in his late 20's and early '30 for age, he was a Deputy Sheriff of Waseca County, and living in Wilton Township, just west of the community of Otisco.

According to my grandfather's letter, it seemed that the Khanke boys, as they were known, decided to rob the First State Bank of Waseca, upon common knowledge at the time that the famed vault within the bank was under renovation and that a smaller, portable Victor Safe would be put in place for the time being until such alterations could be made to the main vault. This two week process would not take long and with a Victor Safe in place, valuables were kept well protected.

What the Khanke brothers did not know at the time was that this information was a ruse, put out by the Sheriff's Department, specifically my grandfather Rathkey, to flush them out, once and for all, and put them behind bars for the crimes they were suspected of committing but never proven as such. Grandfather lived in the Wilton area, and had 5 acres of land purchased along the Wilton River, so he had a vested interest in keeping people safe and the territory clear of these bad ombres.

Well, the ruse almost worked, except that the Saturday night of the robbery in the late spring of the year the Khanke brothers, already deciding to use dynamite to blow the back door and remove the safe via a horse and wagon rather than try a safe cracking method inside the bank where the overnight guard was on duty, revised their plan on the run. Turns out the private security guard, having been from out of town and with lesser known credentials than his predecessor, was one of the Khanke cousins and simply opened the back door to facilitate his kin in their quest for deposits.

The safe was loaded onto a wagon pulled by two farm draft horses and no one was the wiser until it was reported early Monday morning when the bank opened for business. Both Victor Safe and the bank overnight security guard were long gone, and there was egg on the face of the Sheriff's Department for having agreed to such a plan in the first place. Nothing was ever found, no monies recovered, and no safe discovered.

Until later on that winter.

Turns out my grandfather took this robbery personally, and one brisk winter morning set out on his horse for the Otisco area in Wilton where the Khanke brothers were known to hang out. But on his way south of town, having correctly deduced that the brothers would have taken the back roads that early spring night and not old highway 13, started crossing the Wilton River, which ran through the 5 acres of land that grandfather owned, and stopped in the middle of the bridge.

He was looking at various sets of tracks left in the mud from the weekend snow and interpreted what they meant. He knew it was many months since the robbery, but still...something was gnawing at him to keep on the trail. It was then that he looked over the side of the wooden, rickety bridge, looked under the span of the bridge, and saw a wheel sticking up a few inches through the ice that had formed across the Wilton River.

It seemed to be a metal wheel, locked in place, as if it belonged to...

No...could it be?

By God Almight....it was! Even upside down he could tell it was a safe...a Victor Patent safe...and dollars to doughnuts it was from the robbery at the First State Bank of Waseca many months prior. It had been covered by the rising river in the spring, going unnoticed for all these months until the winter ice and lowering river surge showed what it held.

According to his letter, he climbed down the relatively shallow incline, ascertained that his hunch about it being a safe seemed correct, and went back up to get his lariat and threw a lasso out, catching the wheel, and tying off the end to his horse, eased the safe out of the frigid water and onto the banks of the Wilton River.

Keeping the safe well hidden under some cut branches and fir clippings, he hightailed it back into town to the Sheriff's Office (no cell phones back then, folks!), told them of his findings, and together with a four man posse rode back to the Wilton location, this time with more horses, more manpower, and a wagon, to retrieve the now secured safe and bring it back to Waseca.

The safe was kept for evidence for a few months, but all that time in the water had messed up the mechanics necessary for it to still be considered fireproof, waterproof (which it was proven it was not due to being upside down in the Wilton River!) and burglar proof (which it was proven that it was). Seems the Khanke boys had tried to dynamite the safe open, and when that failed, not having any nitroglycerin available to use, decided to abandon the efforts and just get rid of the damn thing once and for all.

But the magnanimous owners of the bank, along with the Board of Directors, directed the bank to dispose of the now useless safe and order a new version of the Victor Safe…one that would be bolted to the floor should such emergencies be ordered for in the future. That left the bank to 'dispose' of the old Victor Safe in whatever manner they seemed appropriate…and their pleasure at having the safe returned in the first place by my grandfather seemed to be the logical place to have it reside, should my grandfather so wish.

OK…so what does one do with a 400# portable sate that will not open?

Well…you take it to a proper gunsmith or locksmith that has the appropriate skill set and training and tools and you have him remove the interlocking floor plate (something not known or advertised to the general public), thaw things out and in this case, really just let air do it's 'thing' and over time….viola!!!! The combination will eventually work, you can open the safe, and find the original contents at the time of the robbery, which were…

NOTHING! Like I said, according to grandfather's letter, the Victor Safe was a ruse, but that was only known to the bank president and the Sheriff's Department...no one else.

But all's well that ends well, as the safe was now in working order and would be for many years to come. The Khanke brothers had moved on further west to the Wells area (great…one of grandfather's brothers lived in that area…good luck to them with getting past his sense of duty and righteousness!)

But that still didn't answer the question of 'Why' was I left the safe, and in particular this letter? Because there was one clue on the outside of the safe that grandfather Rathkey 'assumed' that at least one of the Rathkey kids would either ask about one day or try to figure out, and he wanted to 'set the record straight' since he was in direct knowledge of the accurate information from the get-go.

That 'set the record straight' quote from grandfather's letter would come back to my ears many times from the 1950's up through the mid 1990's…my fathers words to the tee! Now I know where he originally got it.

Like father, like son!

As it turns out, the serial number of the Victor Safe was stamped into the backside of the portable safe, with each safe having its' own unique number for purposes of identification, for purposes just like the bank robbery for proving provenance.

The serial number at the back of the safe was on record as 'having been stolen' and those records still existed, and not updated, which means technically…I was now in possession of an illegal safe used in the robbery of The First State Bank of Waseca back in the late 1890's.

Except I had the letter of exoneration that would prove that while it was in my possession, it also proved that its' trip along the way was legal and above board and nothing nefarious was in play here.

I thank my grandfather for writing this letter and placing it in the safe, if not for me to find someday at least for a sibling or another worthy soul to happen upon. And leaving the skeleton key with a trusted family friend, Floris Splitter, over the years to secure it's identity…priceless. I only wish she could have been available to listen to my reading of the letter once I found it. But I have a feeling that she already knew the contents of the letter way before my time.

Thanks, Floris…your memory is truly that of a good friend, to my family and to me.

But…

While that one skeleton key…one of the 'twins'… and letter behind a locked cubby hole in the Victor Safe answered one question, several still remained.

And those two questions are the most pressing of this entire mystery.

There was a 'second' skeleton key…pressed into my hand on the very night at Lakeshore Inn Nursing Home at the passing of my mother…that was identical to the first skeleton key that Floris Splitter had given me in a letter. Both were copies of the insignia of the Victor Patent safe, both bent at about a 15 degree angle and skeleton in nature…but there was only one problem:

There was only one locked cubby hold in the Victor safe, and that locked cubby hold was already opened and the contents revealed…the story behind the safe, the robbery of the bank by the Khanke brothers, the finding of the safe by my grandfather Rathkey, and his subsequent possession and ownership of said safe until it was passed on to my father, then on to me at his passing in 1996.

There would be no need for a 2nd skeleton key for the same cubby hole, unless…

Now I needed to go back and do some homework. The game that I thought was solved is still afoot.

And Sherlock Rathkey needs to respond!

It has been a few days since my last entry above, relative to the letter left to me by my grandfather, and I can now say with certainty…'yes, there were 2 identical skeleton keys'…and 'yes,…

I know why'.

For someone with such a brilliant mind such as myself, and with my photographic and eidetic memory talents, you would think all it takes for me is a few second to think back to the past, be it way back or merely yesterday, and come up with a solution.

But 'it' does not work that way.

Besides 'seeing' something, and then remembering it, it also has to be in some sort of 'context'; there has to be some meaning for it to stick to my memory banks.

And it took some more research on the Victor Safe and Lock Company out of Cincinnati, Ohio for me to come up with what had been in front of me all along!

When one opens up the Victor Safe door, after turning the combination dial several times in both right and left directions, you pull on the outside handle and the door will open approximately 90 degrees on two, very strong rotating hinges. The safe is relatively fireproof, waterproof (huh!!! Proved that one wrong!) and burglar proof.

But it also has a hidden compartment, known only to the original owner and with a locked entrance for purposes of hidden identity and security as well as secrecy.

It seems that on 'special' models of the Victor Safe, not advertised to the general public but to 'special' buyers such as precious metals buyers, precious stones buyers, banks and securities companies…you get the idea...there is an 'added feature' that only the primary purchaser is aware of.

There is a 2nd, locked compartment, located on the inside of the outside door, that can only be accessed by adjusting the opened door another 10 degrees back towards the close, then extending it further open another 25 degrees to the right to expose the locked compartment hidden in the doorway.

You cannot see this locked compartment upon normal opening and closing of the door, and you cannot open it without knowing the precise degree measurements you need to carefully take when accessing the ability to open it further.

Looking at the safe head on, from the outside, you would think nothing is out of the ordinary. But you will notice that the combination is off-set to the left of center, with the inner tumbler workings all bearing to the left of center inside the door.

And it is to the right of that combination turn, on the inside of the door, that you will find the hidden compartment…and accessed only by the use of a 2nd identical skeleton key, a 'twin' if you will to the first key used in the cubby hole compartment.

This was the key my mother pressed into my hand the night of her passing, but there is more to the story.

You see, back in 1998, the night of her passing, as I entered LakeShore Inn Nursing Home and proceeded down the hall to my mother's room, where my sister was waiting for me just outside her door, another nursing attendant was leaving my mothers room, putting her left hand in her front apron pocket as she kept her head down and passed me in the hall. I thought for a briefest of moments that she looked familiar, but I might have been mistaken as my mind was focused on what lay ahead of me, lying in a bed with only moments of life left in her body.

Upon hindsight, the twin skeleton key that was pressed into my hand by my mother was given to her just seconds before by the woman that was seen leaving her room…Floris Splitter!

That's where I had seen the face before… I at first thought it was Doris Splitter, Dr. Hampton's nursing attendant and secretary, but it was her twin sister, as Doris had since passed away.

Floris had gone into my mother's room and unbeknownst to me, gotten the 2nd skeleton key from my mother's valet located on the top of her dresser and pressed it into her hands, telling her that 'Donny was on his way' and would be there shortly.

These were the same words my sister shared with me when we talked after Mom had passed away and we were revisiting her last few hours. It was as if Pauline, and later on, Floris, had helped 'will' Mom to live for just a few more minutes, as I was traveling from west central Minnesota to Waseca, and the trip would take me several hours to complete.

But I was on my way, and both of them helped keep Mom alive if for no other reason than to give her reason to fight to see me one more time, even though it was clear that she was blind at the time of her passing. She did not 'see' the key Floris put in her hand, that would later be put in mine, but I am sure she knew the significance of it.

And so the journey continues.

But what was in that secret, second compartment of the Victor Safe, that my mother held the key to and was passed on to me? It is now almost 27 years later and to what significance would there be found?

Just as was stated several times in one of my favorite Broadway musicals, 'Phantom of the Opera'…'Look here…I have a note'!

Yes, there was a note.

Only this note, while addressed to 'Donny Rathkey or descendant', was more of a financial plan and accounting notice, it held my intrigue to the point where my mouth was agape and my tongue falling out of my mouth like a yellow lab waiting to retrieve a mallard drake in the sloughs north of Waseca!

I scanned the older, crusty note, which was more notes than text, until I grasped exactly what I was holding on to. I called for Julie, gave her the "Cliff Notes' version of what I had been up to, and then showed her what I had found hidden in the 2nd, sealed compartment of the Victor Safe.

She scanned the material, looked at me, and suddenly began to weep, as did I, for we both suddenly realized the real impact of what we had just found was going to have not only on our lives but that of our daughters, their significant others, our five grandchildren, and possibly…generations to come.

To put it briefly, what I had discovered was the origination of a 'constantly revolving and escalating investment portfolio' that had been originally established back in 1935…90 years ago…just a few days after the marriage of my mother and father Rathkey. I was holding onto a document that was originated almost 100 years ago, was original in its' form and function, and was legally binding, according to all of the legal stamps and verifications we found along with it.

And this is what it said:

On August 1, 1935, my parents, Leon and Irma Rathkey, along with my maternal grandfather, Warren Scarton; paternal grandparents, Hans and Izzy Rathkey; and my god parents, Lee and Bea Rolofson…those 7 people had established four trust funds: one for each of the yet unconceived, unborn, unnamed children that Leon and Irma 'planned' on having.

Holy crap on a cracker…talk about advanced planning directives!

The trusts were simply named after 'Baby 1', 'Baby 2', Baby 3' and 'Baby 4' with names to be given to the written documents after which each child was born. Each trust fund would have 1 principal overseer, with each of the above mentioned families having one voice over one child, should those plans need to be revoked, as outlined below.

The purpose of the trust funds were laid out: Each of the aforementioned planned children would have a trust fund established in the amount of a $10,000 investment and would be able to collect such proceeds from the trust fund AFTER first graduating from an accredited College or University, payable and redeemable on said graduation date, and for purposes of establishing their professional role in society. Said child will be made aware of the existence of such trust fund at the start of their senior year in college, but not before, with no access to such funds until the day of graduation. Failure to follow these instructions explicitly will result in the revocation of all such monies earned in said trust funds and forfeited back to the original principals of said trust funds upon demand.

You've got to be shitting me?

My ancestors set up trust funds for down the road, before me or any of my siblings were even conceived, for purposes of bettering our lives in a yet uncertain world.

There is no way in hell that I could even come up with such a dream plan as this one, but looking back, at the character of those individuals, I can see how it happened. These folks all came up through the depression, with ancestral immigrants coming from ravaged areas of Europe, to settle in America with hopes of a better tomorrow for their kin and children.

Talk about the American dream in reality!

But let's get to reality and what this really spells out for me and my siblings.

My oldest brother, Bob, was born two years later, in 1937, and graduated from the University of Minnesota in 1959. Older brother, Terry, was born in 1941 and graduated from the University of Chicago in 1963. Older sister, Pauline, was born in 1947 and graduated from the University of Minnesota in 1969. And bring up the rear was me, Donny, born in 1953 and graduating from the University of Minnesota in 1975 with my first undergrad degree.

That meant that older brother Bob had a trust fund in place for 24 years before accessing it; older brother Terry for 28 years; older sister Pauline for 34 years; and me for.....holy crap on a cracker!...40 years!

I had...repeat...back in 1975 had a trust fund for 40 years that I did not know about! I was never told at the beginning of my senior year that there was a trust fund in existence, and was never given access to nor the proceeds from said trust fund upon my graduation in 1975.

Whiskey Tango Foxtrot!!!!!!!

What in sam hill was going on? Why was I left out of the ballpark?

Well, in deference to my parents, evidently things were a little 'dicey' financially around those times and Leon and Irma were not sure if they would have to dip into that trust fund, of which they were the legal principals, or if they could avoid it. You need to remember that my parents, while marrying young, had me very late…Dad was 44 years old and Mom was 38 at the time of my birth. That also means that working options for an older man were very limited as both he and I got older, and with Mom not working outside of the home except for 'odd' days at the Waseca Sports Shop in the late 1950's before Dad sold out in 1960, income was limited for the family and needs or desires of the 'runt of the litter', so to speak.

So no one said a word. Not my parents, not my god parents, not my siblings. My grandparents were all passed on by then, and with me having no knowledge about said trust fund, no one was the wiser.

But my folks seemed to stabilize their situation and over the next several years when I started my professional career in the field of education and administration and being a family man, well, things just seemed to get put on a back burner and left there.

To just smolder, or simmer, or whatever the proper term is for forgetting about something…until it is too late and there is no one there to fill in the blanks.

But here we are, in 2025, and I am sitting on a trust fund that has been rolling over and accumulating wealth and increasing automatically on a yearly basis and now has come the time to actually 'know' what has been lying dormant for the past almost 90 years and is now going to be brought to life in the modern world.

Putting it bluntly, my 'invisible' financial advisor who has been overseeing this wealth investment and accumulation over the past several years, and then passed on to his daughter to oversee, was a long time family friend and confidant of my grandfather, father, and now me, as his daughter and I were close friends growing up and went to college together...but was never told of the 'secret' she was keeping from me all these years.

Turns out my trust fund included not only money, but stocks, bonds, self maturing and roll-over treasury notes, precious stones like diamonds, rubies, garnets, sapphires and precious metals like gold, silver, titanium, and palladium.

My particular trust fund, started in 1935, and for the first 40 years until the 'established' date of relinquishment, rolled over or doubled 8 times during that 40 year period. Translation: if $1 had been the original investment amount, it would roll over to 2, then 4, then 8, then 16, then 32, then 64, then 128, and finally to 256...$256 for each $1 initial investment.

But the original trust fund investment set up for 'Baby 4'... me...was not $1; It was $10,000, same as everyone else's.

So upon my graduation from the U of M, I had $2.56 million sitting in a trust fund I knew nothing about!

Now, let's work those numbers ahead some more. In the next, and last, 50 years, from 1975 until today in 2025, that same amount of money has rolled over, or doubled, a total of 7 times. That means the investment of $2.56 million from 1975 grew to an amount that today sits at $327,680,000 million!

You gotta be kidding me! That's right up there 'in the Rockefeller neighborhood', as my Dad would say!

Now one has to remember that about half, around 50%, of that investment income is not mine...it belongs, rightfully so, to the Federal Government and the Internal Revenue Service in the form of taxes, as does part of it belong to the State of Minnesota and the Department of Revenue. But I think with even the big boys getting their fair share of the earnings, there is still plenty enough for me and my family to not only live off of but do something that my ancestors did for me:

Invest in the future of our families…and that would be my daughters and grandchildren, and possibly even great grandchildren that are not even on anyone's radar at this point in time. I have to do the 'right thing', even in light of some upcoming information that will shake this family to its' very foundation.

I still need to do the right thing.

And with Julies' help and support, which I know I already have, it will be done.

As was stated earlier by Ramses…'so let it be written, so let it be done'.

But now we come to the 'final' piece of the puzzle, well, at least this puzzle…and that deals with my existence and what really happened during the early morning hours of that stormy day back on October 6, 1953.

And that is where a letter, originated by my grandfather Rathkey but also initialed by my mother and father on the outside of that envelope at a later date, was found in the bottom of that Victor Safe.

We found the 1st secret the safe revealed, the origination of the origins of the safe in grandfather Rathkey's possession. That secret was found after using a skeleton key, kept by an old family friend, in the sealed cubby hold in the top of the safe.

We found the 2nd secret the safe revealed, the origination of the trust fund established by early ancestors on my behalf, and the values of that said trust fund today. Again, the secret was found after using a skeleton key, the 'twin' to the 1st, kept by the same old family friend and given to my mother the night of her passing to give to me in her final moments here on earth.

Such a gift…no words can adequately describe.

But now the safe will give up its' 3rd and final secret…an envelope, addressed to me in the handwriting of my grandfather but initialed on the back at some later date by Leon and Irma Rathkey, to be opened by me upon finding.

Though, I have to admit, hiding it under the existing carpet, or adding the carpet as an additional layer of protection and hiding it better made for a rather difficult find.

But this was not only the letter of a lifetime, it was the 'find' of a lifetime.

And now is the time for that final reveal to occur.

According to the letter written by my grandfather Rathkey, several things happened the night of, the early morning of, and since that date of October 6, 1953. The letter was written by my grandfather Rathkey, as he and Irma were very close, with Irma having lost her own mother when Irma was only 11 years old and losing her father later on in the early 1940's, just a few short years after marrying Leon. She leaned on her father in law, and he in turn provided fatherly advice. And they were solid as a team.

And as my father, and soon to be found out grandfather Rathkey would say…'when you have the chance to set the record straight, you set the record straight.' I would expect nothing less of a former Deputy Sheriff of Waseca County…both of them.

Well, that solidness was going to be put to the test the morning of October 6th. It seems that in all of the confusion of the storm and power outages and personnel shortages at Waseca Memorial Hospital, no one was 'really' in charge of what was going on which allowed for some irregular and nefarious activities to take place over the course of a few short hours.

First Irma was brought in during the very early morning hours, already in labor, and in severe pain, enough so that an IV was set up and morphine administered to help calm her down and get her ready for delivery. But at the same time a transcient young girl, later proven out to be a wayward 'tramp' with unknown origin, wandered in off the street after being dropped off by an old jalopy and she, too, was in the early stages of labor.

Both females occupied the same room in the upper floors of the hospital, as personnel was lacking due to a shortage and power was not available. Even the surgical suite downstairs was temporarily moved upstairs, and would be in use a few hours later due to Judge Noolen coming in for emergency surgery, which could only be performed by Dr. Cecil Hampton, the only licensed physician on staff and available at the time, though he was also tending to both pregnant ladies as best he could. He had assistance from his nursing team, consisting of Doris Splitter and an intern, but that was it....personnel shortage all over the hospital and gaps in not only support but coverage and oversight to the point where the left hand did not know what the right was doing.

Well, Mrs. Rathkey did not react well to the morphine and soon slipped into a state of unconsciousness. Still breathing on her own, she was only a short time away from full labor and giving birth, and Dr. Hampton was attending to the Judge at that very moment.

Add to that the same condition for the incoming 'Jane Doe' and that birthing room was a complete disaster. An IV was set up and morphine administered to the young girl, but her condition was fading fast as she was having a negative reaction to the morphine...but there was no one around to assist her directly as she slipped and slipped and slipped further away with each succeeding moment.

The moment of delivery came quickly for Mrs. Rathkey, and at 7:26 am she gave birth to a 7#, 12 oz baby boy, according to the birth certificate signed by Dr. Cecil Hampton and attested to by Ben Frapke, Clerk of Court, on October 15, 1953 and signed by James Fillpot, attestant, and Nellie Day Deputy Clerk of Court on said date.

Yup...that's what the official Certificate of Birth says, and I am looking at a signed copy of said certificate in my hands as I write.

Yup...that's what it says.

But that's not what happened.

The 'official' version, as reported by my grandfather and would later be backed up by DNA testing in an Oregon lab by cousin Desiree Spoettcher, is a little different story.

Irma Rathkey did give birth at 7:26 am on October 6, 1953… to a stillborn baby girl, deformed and badly misfigured. Mrs. Rathkey was not in a coma or completely unconscious during delivery, but she was so 'out of it' that she could not speak, nor react to any stimulus given. Her labor and subsequent birthing procedure went very quickly, and the fetus remained between her legs for only a few minutes before being attended to.

That's good…'cause there was no stimulus to be given by anyone because there was no one else in the room except for 'Jane Doe' in the adjoining bed, also giving birth in an uncontrolled setting with no medical personnel present. Mrs. Rathkey had given birth to a stillborn fetus with no medical personnel present, and 'Jane Doe' was about to do the same thing, only this result would be far different.

'Jane Doe' gave birth to a 7#, 12 oz baby boy, with his lungs crying out for oxygen, at exactly 7:26 am on October 6, 1953…the same time as Mrs. Rathkey's birthing process was completed. But 'Jane Doe' was in dire straights, as she was bleeding uncontrollably from a torn cervix during delivery, an injury that would not be discovered for another 3 minutes and by then, the effects were fatal.

One healthy baby boy, without a living mother, and near death.

One stillborn, deformed fetus, with a living mother, though semi conscious.

Enter Floris Splitter.

Doris's twin sister, Floris, had gotten word about the power outages and personnel shortages and gotten to the hospital as quickly as possible to see if her sister needed any assistance with Dr. Hampton or with any emergencies that had come in. Doris saw her come in, called to her to have to check on the two ladies in the birthing room, and 'take' care of things until she or the good Doctor could come in to finish up.

Floris went into the birthing room at 7:29 am, immediately assessed the situation, and in a single movement of both motherly care and empathetic feelings, cut the umbilical cord of Mrs. Rathkey's deceased baby girl, and wrapped the remains in a covered blanket and put them at the end of the bed holding 'Jane Doe'.

One minute later Floris completed the same procedure with the new born son of 'Jane Doe' and put the blanketed and crying baby in the baby crib at the side of Mrs. Rathkey's bed.

She went over to attend to 'Jane Doe', but it was too late. The blood loss was just too great to sustain life, even if attention had been given sooner. 'Jane Doe' had already expired. Floris pulled up a clean sheet over the head of the deceased woman just as both her twin sister, Doris, and Dr. Hampton entered the birthing room.

It was not hard to ascertain what had happened, and actions were taken quickly to curtail the morphine IV in Mrs. Rathkey and bring her around medically as soon as possible so that she could attend to her new born son.

Attention was also given to 'Jane Doe' so that she was respectfully attended to. An attendant from the hospital holding morgue was summoned and her body was wheeled away and down to the hospital tombs for further examination, if necessary.

Usually in the case of transcients, as little medical attention is provided, other than humanitarian aid, anything considered 'extra' is forgone, as there is no billing partner to seek reimbursement from and with limited resources in the first place, a paupers grave in Wilton Township, the legal resting place of county transcients, would be her final resting place and that of her deceased and deformed daughter.

So one could ascertain that what happened above was 'wrong' on so many levels that we don't know where to start, or some would argue that it was 'right' on so many levels that we can start anywhere and still be wrong.

But what my grandfather Rathkey's letter went on to further

explain, at a later date, was that Mrs. Rathkey was NOT totally 'out of it' when on the morphine IV drip.

She remembered 'Jane Doe' being wheeled in, and while Mrs. Rathkey's eyes belied the fact that she was indeed 'not in a functioning mode' she could in fact see and hear everything that was going on…she just could not move any muscles, facial or otherwise, and react. It was like she was immobilized and in a zombie mode.

Scary!

So Irma, somewhat conscious and visibly watching everything through vacant yet focused eyes, saw the actions Floris took, first with her and later on with 'Jane Doe'. While Mrs. Rathkey could not see at first how stillborn and deformed her baby was (she had no idea it was a girl, at first), she was able to ascertain that from hearing furthering discussions between the three medical personnel as they attended to both her and 'Jane Doe' and a few tears were evident on her pale and clammy face.

And then came the fact that the baby boy crying his lungs out was coming in for breakfast and was not going to stop until he had some. But for some reason, Irma 'shut down' and was not able to feed the new born. As an aside, I remember this story later on as I grew up, my father telling me that I did not 'take' to Mom and that they had me on formula from the 'get go'…which would account for 'why' I was not as big as my older brothers growing up. Older brother Bob was around 6'2" and 200 pounds, while brother Terry was an equal 6'2' and over 220 while in high school.

And then there was Donny. You know that story already, so no need to repeat it here.

So, several days later the Rathkey family went home to North State Street, up at the north end, as there was a new little sheriff in the Rathkey family and it wanted attention. Seems every one was very happy, and a subsequent picture that I remember seeing of Grandfather Rathkey and older sister, Pauline, looking on as grandfather held me, saying 'this is the one…this is the one'.

Ya, well…'this was the one' all right…just not sure which 'one' he was referring to at the time or the one that I would turn out to be years later!

But for some reason, grandfather Rathkey decided it best to put this all in writing a few years later, one year before his own death in 1956. It was a written, documented record of what really happened that morning and the subsequent actions taken to cover up the truth.

This document was in a sealed envelope in the bottom of the safe, and Leon and Irma must have known what the contents were, as they both initialed the backside of the envelope as it to 'support' and 'validate' the contents.

I will never know that, as I am finding this out in 2025 and all other living blood relatives are non existent. I tried to locate just 'who' that transcient girl was back in 1953, but there were no records that I could find that support missing young girls from family homes, group homes, orphanages, church sponsored foster homes…nothing was coming into play. Nothing from missing persons, either from churches, locales, schools….nothing.

It was if a ghost came into view, delivered, then departed this earth in a most unceremoniously way.

Perhaps….not a 'ghost', but rather an 'angel'?

And as for the sperm donor….well, good luck with that one. A 16 year old girl, who could have been 15 at the time of conception, well, remember this was the early 1950's…who knows who or what or when happened or what went on. I sure don't.

All I know is what I discovered in some old written court and medical documents, secreted documents squirreled away in an old family safe, and some oral testimony before some people died.

That's all. That's all that I know, and what I can prove.

But I do know one thing for sure.

While I had no control over the distant past relative to my birth, and no control over events and circumstances absent my own misbehavior during my lifetime, I know what has to be done relative to my future.

There can be only one outcome that is worthy.

There can be only one resolution that is worthy.

But first…first…I have to get past, and bring to light, that awful cloud from the mid 1960's and it's subsequent ending of a few years back.

I have to bring to light what might be remembered as the darkest hours of my life, for only I know what they are.

I know what I did.

I know why I did it.

I believe I was justified in what I did.

But the dead may think otherwise.

21

50TH YEAR REUNION REFLECTIONS: SET UP AND MURDER

Crystal and Waseca, Minnesota
July, 2021...and sometime before that

> The German philosopher Friedrich Nietzsche gave a stern warning to those of us who confront the worst that we do to each other. 'Whoever fights monsters should see to it that in the process he does not become a monster. And if you gaze long enough into an abyss, the abyss will gaze back into you.' It's a warning we would do well to heed. Empathy is a necessary tool but we have to guard against the horrors we see becoming our new normal.
>
> From 'Reading Crimes' by Dr. Tony Hill

Oh, to have only read those words long ago, and then again in the not too distant past, perhaps some of my demons would not have been fed so eagerly or so easily as they were. One always has some regrets in life, and while most are regrettable, there is always one that will stand out and defy all that you hold dear, something that you hang on to for all that it is worth, in the name of justice and truth and humanity.

Such was the case with Donny, but this story actually begins many, many decades ago in the halls of Waseca Central High School during his junior high days of 1965-68, then skipping ahead a few decades to its' final resolution...or should I say the 'final' resolution for one of the main principals?

As you have previously read, Donny had a somewhat checkered past, both inside and outside of school and home. Behaviors all over the place, hormones and actions racing between that which is right and that which is easy, and always...always...the negative and often aggravating reactions to any form of injustice that was being done to another, friend or foe made no difference. And in the case we are about to analyze, we will see that while Donny thought he was in the 'right' for much of the reactionary time, we will leave that final judgement to the people reading and responding to his story.

But it begins early and throughout his first year in high school, 1965-1966. Donny, in his usually tormenting manner, would evoke the most negative responses from other kids...usually boys...that teased him for various reasons, but usually associated with clothes he was wearing, personal hygiene (or the lack thereof), im-maturing social skills, and physical reactions to these negative behaviors that only invited more of the same, and usually in escalating mannerisms. There were no swear words that he didn't know and use, there were no obscene gestures that he didn't know how to show, and there were no methods to his brazen attempts at recognition, though they usually be misguided and ill conceived.

The same was true as his 8th grade year would role around, and the above mentioned behaviors were only getting worse and more obvious to those around him, be it student or teacher.

Or at home...his parents. Leon and Irma were trying their darndest, but as Donny's behaviors seemed to get more pronounced and frequent, the physical and verbal reactions of his parents seem to cause an intolerance to develop within his psyche and made him impervious to pain and any subjugation of punishment or discipline. The Rathkey's were growing older by the day, and their efforts to rein in their youngest were becoming tantamount to draining a swamp during a time when it rained every single day.

They tried, he resisted, and life went on.

But in the spring of Donny's freshman year, 1968, in early May, Donny's older brother, Terry, himself a 1959 graduate of the same high school, came to school and presented to an all school assembly a program revolving around the VISTA program...a government sponsored program called 'Volunteers in Service to America.' The audience of over 800 students in grades 7-12, along with faculty and staff, were genuinely interested in hearing what he had to say, as he himself was involved as a participant and later on a spokesperson for a program that advocated helping out your fellow humanity in efforts other than options provided for by the military.

The spring of 1968 was a particularly volatile time in America in general, as the Viet Nam war (or conflict, whatever your 'correct' political preference might be) was in full swing, the military draft was functioning as it was supposed to, and bodies were being brought back home to all 50 states due to the loss of young life in a conflict that many believe we had no business being involved in in the first place.

But, be that as it may, Terry's presentation was well received... by most, but not all.

And it was 2 of the 'not all' minority that decided the time had come for a reckoning to be made of the youngest Rathkey kid... the one with the funny clothes, big mouth, pimply face, and hot shot temper that needed to be put in his place.

You see, all during Donny's upper elementary and junior high days Donny had been tormented by older students that liked to make fun of younger students, Donny included. They would taunt and ridicule, and Donny, and others, would respond in kind by swearing at them, flipping them off, questioning their mother's backgrounds….you get the idea. It usually resulted in running away, to home; or being shoved into a locker; or having your books slapped from your hands, making you late for your next class. Always the same old bullshit, but not answering the age old question:

What came first: the teasing and taunting, or the swearing and flipping off of the bird?

Well, it really didn't matter, as this revolving behavioral door continued from grades 5 and 6 up through grades 7, 8, and 9… until one afternoon in May of 1968 when it all came to a head.

After the morning assembly in the auditorium, as Donny was walking down the second floor stairs toward the lunchroom in the basement of the high school for lunch, he was confronted by two of his major upperclassmen nemesis…seniors Greg Schister and his sidekick, Tim Mallberg.

They started teasing Donny about his 'draft dodging' brother and how he kept from serving his country by 'dodging' his rightful duty to serve in the military, and instead opted for the 'soft' life of serving the indigenous Indian population of the great southwest. They continued to taunt him as they went downstairs, passing several teachers on the way who did not step in or try to alter the course of misbehavior they were witnessing. Books were knocked from hands, words were spoken, 'birds' flew, and the next thing Donny knew, he had accepted a challenge to meet Schister after school on the southside playground area in front of school for a fight.

Whiskey Tango Foxtrot!

What have I just gotten myself into? Physically, I was about 5'9", 140 pounds wringing wet, and I was going up against a brute that was about 6" taller and carried another 60 pounds over me on his lanky frame. Picture David and Goliath. And worse of all, he seemed more motivated to send me to the promised land than I did in trying to defend not only my brother's honor but the Rathkey name, in general.

Well, as you can guess, lunch did not sit very well and neither did my afternoon classes. I was nervous, to be perfectly honest, and to really lay it on thc line…this was going to be my 1st fight in which I was not only the underdog by a huge margin, there was no margin to even be given.

I knew a few moves from having been taught by Dad down in the storeroom with an old pair of maroon boxing gloves back a few years when I was younger, but that was mostly 'play' with no serious directions being given…just a few tips on what to protect and how to avoid a direct hit to the old noggin.

Well, the 3:00 pm bell rang and I had no sooner made my way back to my locker and down the hall when I started hearing the jeers from other students, even before I hit the doors to go outside to the south side asphalt playground area next to the grassy square on the main, front side of school on facing Elm Avenue.

I had been in contact that afternoon with a friend and classmate, Dan Mueller, who was walking with me and being supportive of my efforts, but he was mostly there to hold my glasses when this fiasco got underway. Dan was a grandson of a family friend, Gordy Mueller, who lived across the alley behind the Waseca Sports Shop, a business my father used to own in the late 1950's. We went to the same church, knew the same people, and generally hung out together, as he also had a penchant for pushing bullies back when confronted with their negative behaviors.

As you can tell, I am not very confident in how this ruse is going to play out, but I did not feel like I had a choice to 'turn the other cheek' and walk away, as the taunting that would come after than would be far worse than facing the music and meeting this bully head on, toe to toe, in the place of his choosing.

By the time I got to the grassy area of the playground, there was already a crowd of about 50-100 students that had formed somewhat of a circle, and guess who was in the middle, already raising his hands in a 'rocky-type' victory salute...even before we started. I made my way to the middle, glared at this behemoth before me, and made a critical mistake one learns to NEVER EVER make when getting ready to fight.

I turned my back to Schister, so that I could hand my glasses over to Dan, who was standing to my right. No use having busted glasses added to the damage that was about to be inflicted, and possibly one less thing my parents, especially my mother, could bitch about once I got home.

Well, as soon as I turned my head and took off my glasses, but BEFORE I could fully hand them off to Dan, I was pummeled by a hard sucker punch blow to the back of my head near my left ear, a blow that would drop me to my knees. I hit the ground, was pushed to my right onto my back, and the blows from Schister's fists were raining down like claps of thunder.

...right...left...right...left....right...right...

And there was not a damn thing I could do. I was outweighed, out positioned, and my arms were locked under his body, which was sitting on my chest as he wailed away. I briefly caught site of something, but I don't remember what...but I seem to remember another senior boy stepping in to stop the fight and call it 'over'.

But that was just before Schister's sidekick, Mallberg, decided a kick to my head while I was down and 'out of it' was something he needed to do for his 'part' in this ambush.

And then it must have been over.

I don't know, as I don't recall anything after that, other than waking up, rolling over, and feeling like shit. My glasses lay beside me on the ground, next to me, but unbroken. But my head not only felt like a mess, the blood on my shirt indicated that something was a mess and I needed to find out what it was.

I raised myself up, slowly, only to find that there were no school busses around, no other kids on the playground, no others looking out from the school windows. I had no idea of time, no idea of how long I had lain there, no idea of anything, other than an urge to get to the boys locker room to try and clean up before going home.

Guess I was not going to track practice today.

I limped back into the school; actually, I slouched going back in, somewhat limping but not due to an injured hip or leg but in trying to keep my head down so anyone in the hallway would not see me enter the building. I made my way to the locker room, saw myself in the mirror, and slowly gasped at what was looking back at me.

I grabbed a towel from the rack and tried to get it somewhat wet so I could wipe some of the blood off my messed up face, which at this time was getting colored in addition to hurting like hell. In the coaches locker room I noticed the clock on the wall indicating it was around 3:30 pm, and head track coach Benny Mackmann was putting his whistle around his neck, getting ready for track practice. He looked at me, shook his head, and walked out of the coaching room, through the locker room, and out the north door to drive down to the track for practice.

Some role model, huh?

Oh, well…we all have to answer someday, and his day will come.

After a few minutes I decided to gather up my things from my locker and walk to the fire station, as I knew Dad was working that day. He had told me a few days prior that he would be unable to attend the spring musical concert that evening since he was on duty and…

Holy crap on a cracker!

Tonight was the spring musical concert…and I had to sing with the choir!

Oh, damn…damn….damn. This is not gonna be good.

I hurried to gather my things together and walked as quickly as I could, using the back streets to get to the fire station and confront my father. Dad met me at the door, and indicated that he had just gotten 'word' of a dust-up after school that involved me.

Well, one look at my face would have told you that.

So, he put his arm around me and without saying a word, brought me in, sat me down, and used some materials from the first aid kit to stem some of the bleeding that was still occurring and to patch me up somewhat so that I looked more 'presentable' when I walked home to see Mom.

Yup…gonna have to walk another 9 blocks home, after walking 5 blocks here, and get another dose of 'something' that as of yet, I had no idea what it would be..

After Dad got things more under control, at least as well as he could, I explained as best I could what had transpired, all the way from earlier taunting and my reactions to that crap (tried to play the 'victim' card, but not sure it worked as well as I would have liked) and then filled him in on the things that happened today, from Terry's VISTA assembly to the taunting and challenge afterwards, to the fight.

Well, not much of a fight from my side of things. But even though I was ambushed and sucker punched from behind when my back was to my tormentor, I was raised in a 'turn the other cheek' household, and when that was the word, that was the final word…no questions asked. Wish I had learned to ask questions better when younger!

Well, sometimes when you turn the other cheek you are going to get the shit kicked out of you…like it or not, rules or not, philosophy or not, teachings or not. And that is what happened today, and now I had to deal with the ramifications of that altercation both at home and at school.

Dad listened to me, offered words of encouragement, wondering if he needed to 'step in' and take care of things, and I said 'no'...that would only make things worse at school. So I picked my things up and walked home, though I seemed to be walking more slowly, for I knew what was awaiting me at home, and the price I was going to have to pay for my part on this fight was going to hurt more than the beating I took at the hands of the bully Schister and Mallberg.

But when I got home, both my mother, in tears, and my older brother, Terry...the look in his eyes would have melted steel... greeted me with hugs and brought me inside to have further tending to do on my wounds and cuts and bruises.

Seems Dad had called ahead, informed Mom of the situation but also leaned heavily on the 'defending my brother's honor' side of things and to take it easy on me, especially with the concert in only a few hours back at the high school.

That was the first, and I think the only, time that I was introduced to foundation and other make-up tricks that my mother used to cover up the bruising on my face so that I was somewhat more presentable at the concert which by now is only an hour away.

My older brother accompanied Mom, since Dad had to work his shift at the fire station, and for some reason, when we got to school the choir members were deafly quiet when I entered the choir room prior to the concert.

And for another 'strange' reason, I was 'moved' from the center of the choir, back row, to the end of the back row, next to where our choir director stood for introductions. Found out later that two things happened that evening prior to me getting to the concert: first of all, the parents of my 'buddy' Dan grounded him from attending the concert that evening and participating, which automatically lowered his grade one letter for missing the concert (he was grounded for not stepping up and in to help his friend); and secondly, the choir director checked with the lighting crew to lighten the electrical bulb load to my end of the back row so that my injuries were not as evident to the average person sitting in the auditorium audience.

I also remember receiving a lot of 'way to go, Butch', 'way to step up', and 'atta boy, Tiger' and slaps on the back…boys and girls, included…as the evening went on during our down time between choir performances. Seems word got out about the 'Thursday after school massacre' and it ended up with Schister and his buddy, Mallberg, being suspended 3 days for fighting on school grounds, and had to live with the scorn and embarrassment that accompanied their ambush of me on the high school playground that afternoon.

Well…while you would think I was now a 'bigger man on campus' for standing up to the bullies of the senior class, I paid a price for that encounter. But the price I would pay psychologically over the next few decades, with that being the initial point of reference, would finally reach a boiling point with me and me alone deciding further actions were warranted to 'set the record straight' against the continued aggression from bullies that didn't learn their lessons earlier in life.

And that time was going to be now.

Fast forward a few decades…we are now a few years older, and as for me, a lot smarter (well, at least on the surface I was smarter) and a whole lot different in terms of physical development.

I was always an underachiever in my younger days. The bar was always set higher than I thought I could reach or attain, so I didn't try as hard as I should have. That feeling of inadequacy followed me not only in the classroom but also in the athletic arena. While the athletic part started to come around, as you read earlier about my outstanding high school accomplishments, the academic part seemed to take a little bit more time.

But it was the maturity and psychological and emotional aspects of my development that really took longer to develop (for many reasons, according to the advisors and counselors that I would see over the years) and when those three areas are not in sync, all areas are not in sync.

Even though my physical presence was now something to take note of, being 6'1" and 275 pounds, dry as a light bulb and quick as a fart, I did not have to use that presence or those attributes as frequently as one might expect of a husband, a father, a grandfather, a school building and district administrator.

But that does not mean that dormant skills are not there. They are just that...dormant... until the right time and place and motivations cause them to be awoken.

Well, by fast forwarding a few decades and learning about some very costly and horrific behaviors exhibited by my former high school bullies Schister and Mallberg, still tormenting people, especially women, in the Waseca area and surrounding countryside... well, that just didn't set well with me, especially since one of those assaulted women happened to be an old high school friend that needed a shoulder to lean on and a helping hand to get back on her feet.

So, I decided to take things into my own hands and with the physical and mental skill sets I had developed over the years, along with specialized MA training and covert operations development from my earlier college stint with the FBI, I knew what had to be done, when it had to be done, and how I would do it.

The only question left was: by which method will the lesson be administered?

You see...at that time I was not thinking of this as a 'suicide' mission where not only would I take care of the bullies once and for all but I would sacrifice myself for the 'cause' of justice and honor and truth.

Well, the 'sacrifice' part would have to be hidden and avoided, if at all possible, as I was a husband and father and grandfather and there were others counting of me to be around, not just functionally but in all other manners.

But based on the knowledge that seemed to be commonplace in Waseca, and certainly to me, lack of 'proof' on the part of the Waseca police department and Waseca County sheriff's office was what was causing the delay in apprehending these two scumbags. And the judicial authorities in Waseca County were not going to issue warrants and allow citizens to be apprehended without probable cause and proof to back it up.

With all due respect to those above mentioned three institutions…Police, Sheriff, and Courts…each one made up of fine individuals that support the Constitution and the law as it is written and interpreted…I am more of a 'Jack Reacher' kind of guy, or a 'Cotton Malone' kind of operative.

While words and manuals and common law are great in most instances, sometimes you need to act like Rip and Kevin Costner in 'Yellowstone' and just go out and beat the hell out of someone, separate their living body from their functioning organs, and throw their damn body over the ravine for the scavengers of the earth to live on.

That is the mindset that I have been invaded by and that permeates my thinking at the present, and the path that I must follow to effectively and efficiently eliminate the problems as I see it that lay before me.

But, again…I am faced with a small but calculating dilemma: by which means do I use? Or, will it be a multitude of options that need to be rolled into one?

I decide that the best timing for my plan to go into effect will be the weekend of our 50th high school reunion, held at The Mill in downtown Waseca. There will be much activity with many visitors and spouses coming to town, and that also means much confusion and little attention being paid to things that ought to have been paid attention to. That's where I come in, do the deed or deeds, and slip away knowing none will be the wiser.

'From such crooked wood as that which man is made of, nothing straight can be fashioned.' Immanuel Kant

Damn, son…you keep coming up with these sayings and you might just talk yourself out of doing what you in your heart knows is right to do!

My recollections of the reunion will be brief, much like thought and memories from those high school years. We were joined with the graduating class of 1971 from Sacred Heart High School…the last senior class to graduate from the Catholic school located on the west edge of Waseca and the Class of '71 from Central High School, the last class to graduate from that particular building, as they built a new high school and then a junior high/middle school just north of town further north on Highway 13, just a northerly extension of North State Street where I used to live as a youth.

There were several classmates that I visited with, some more briefly than others and some in more detail than others, at the afternoon get-together out at Clear Lake Park. One of my classmates even brought along his Ruger 9mm with his Conceal and Carry badge stuck to the holster…I left mine in the glove compartment. I didn't even think I needed to 'impress' anyone with those skills, or intents, so I left well enough alone.

I just wanted to be evident, present, but somewhat invisible once this whole reunion thing was over, as my primary reason for being in town was to take care of business, then see old classmates and see how they had aged. Just like people that go to race tracks or watch Nascar on tv….want to see the 'crash', nothing else matters or cares!

The evening at The Mill was a nice time to meet old classmates, if you were into that sort of thing. Seems like more people were respectful of me this time around, for whatever reasons, so it was enjoyable and not just tolerable to be in their presence. There are always gonna be the 'divas' and 'prima donnas' and 'kings of the hill' that need to make their presence known, but once you size them up and realize the fronts they are sprouting, and probably the deceits they are concealing, you soon realize that the only people they are fooling are themselves.

Who cares who screwed the homecoming queen behind the football bleachers or who drank the most Old Milwaukee after the blowout loss to rival Wells in a basketball game? I mean, who really gives a shit?

But it is fun to see how people change, how they either mellow or grow a set, or especially how they have aged over the years. Beauty is skin deep but ugly goes all the way to the bone, or so the saying goes. People that would not give you the time of day 50 years ago treat you like a long lost brother, and some people you are close to maybe want to get closer, but for no apparent reason. Go figure!

But while those social interactions and a buffet meal were occupying our efforts in the early evening, my thoughts had drifted directly to the plan that I had set in motion weeks earlier when I had come to Waseca, under the guise of doing some pre-season scouting for deer hunting for archery season, now only a few weeks away. It was the prefect cover under which I could leave home, be gone for several days, and to do this several times so that my data collected would be reliable when the time came to implement the operation.

And to do it all without leaving a trace that I was even in the area.

Again, I am drawn back to 'which' of the methods I will choose to use, as I have options that are all effective, but they also need to be efficient. I need to be 'in and out' and get the job done without alerting anyone to my presence, my activities, and my departure.

And definitely no clues as to the disappearance of any human remains.

The time has come for these two douchebags to pay for what they have done, going all the way back to the spring of 1968 in a beat-down ambush of a younger and smaller boy to the more modern days of physical abuse and assault of women and not being held to account for those actions.

Judge…jury…executioner. Just like the deer hunting assassin I am.

Damn straight.

Now it's time for court to be in session.

I have options in dealing with these pieces of dirt. One option is to simply walk by them, and while distracting them with one hand, put some tetrahydrozoline (Visine) drops in their daily coffee cups that they get at the local buffet at Cashwise grocery store located on the north end of town in the mall. I know when they go in, I know where they sit, I know their routine after getting their coffee and going back for their plate of food…so it's all good as far as reliable routine.

Putting an ounce or two of the over the counter eyedrops will have them dropping like flies…dead flies…under the guise of a heart attach within 15 minutes, and no one will be the wiser. Walking away after doing the deed and driving back home leaves the body disposal to the locals, and my hands are done regarding any cleanup efforts. Since Mallberg and Schister meet daily to partake in this morning and evening ritual, I have options as to which time I decide to enact the plan. But there is another variable that also comes into play that I need to bank on, and not one I can control.

I know for a fact, after research, that the local Waseca Memorial Hospital…yup, the same place you have read about many chapters before this…does not have in their possession either a gas chromatography machine nor a mass spectrometer, also known collectively in the autopsy world as a 'GS-MS' duo. These machines are routine used in major cities and major crime labs in helping to determine cause of death in cases where there is 'high suspicion' that death is not natural and there needs to be further analysis of what is at play here.

But local, backwoods, rural hospitals like Waseca's does not have the resources to purchase such machines, that may be used once a decade, at best. And to farm out the bodies to a more regional location such as Mankato to the west; St. Cloud or the Twin Cities to the north; or Rochester to the east, well…that will take time and extra expense the city or county just does not budget for, unless an emergency.

And death by Visine eyedrops will not be considered an 'emergency' in anyone's book when these two buzzards drop to the floor. A heart attack and Bob's your uncle! The masking element of this option is foolproof, and as long as Schister goes down first, that is the main ombre I am after. Mallberg will just be a 'surprise present' if he also reaches the end of his lifespan.

Well, that option certainly will get the job done and done effectively. But there is another option which will give them some reason to squirm and pay for their past sins, should I choose to go that route. Perhaps a little self reflection on their naughtiness is just what is needed for some type of repentance prior to their execution…or maybe that is too empathetic to the needs of those involved. I have no qualms about watching them try and weasel out their impending doom, but perhaps it is better to just go in, do the deed, and dispose of things and get the hell out of Dodge.

This option goes back to the use of a key for a late night usage of the meat grinder at the old Lau's Meat Shop out at the north end of town. Old Merv owes Dad many favors over the years for the work Dad did for him, and though both men have since passed, his son, Robby, would be all too glad to help out a chum from 'back in the day' take care of some modern scum, along as it was done neatly and quietly.

Hell, I would even wash down the grinder when completed and cart away the remains to be distributed into the Wilton River area as a sort of 'treat' for the scavengers of the woods to enjoy over the next few weeks. Heck, with coyotes ever present in that neck of the woods, there will be no remains left at all to identify within 48 hours after the initial deposit along the ditch sites.

The only question is how to draw out Schister so that he will not be suspecting of an 'ambush', or to leave his vehicle in a prominent place for identification later on down the road. And the best way to do that is to confront him at his own home in southeast Waseca, when he is alone in the evening and living on a quiet, dead-end street with no visible neighbors for hundreds of yards.

Heck, going up to the door, chloroform cloth in right hand behind my back while I knock with my left…he won't even know who I am when I overtake him at the side entrance. Even if he does not open the door the screen is torn enough to allow for my arm and hand to access his face. Previous scouting of his home indicated a blocked front door and porch area, and his side door is the only egress he has for entrance to and from his place of abode.

He boxed himself in and does not even know it.

Parking a block away and walking back to his home to subdue him, then driving my car back to put him in the trunk and drive to the north end of town and his final disposal site will be easy.

Again, as for Mallberg, if he is not affected in this option, so be it. Turns out that over the years, Mallberg has changed, and for the better, so maybe we just let bygones be bygones and let him live. He found God, married and settled down and became a deacon in the church, and also went to school to enter the crime prevention field…imagine that! He ended up working with Dad at the Sheriff's office and became a favorite of his over the years.

Damn, son…you just can't make this shit up! So if this has ended up being his path, so be it. Live and let live…but I bet he will 'get the picture' when he finds out his old high school buddy has suddenly decided that perhaps Waseca is not for him anymore!

After much thought over the first two options, while workable, I have decided on a more prudent option, at least prudent for me. I know that fishing is a desired hobby of Schister, and that he routinely likes to go out on Loon Lake at the west end of town and fish for small mouth bass and panfish, something the lake has in abundance His fishing partner just happens to be the town drunk, old Charlie Johnson, who like Schister, will do just about anything for a free beer and a chaser...and a few bucks.

So old Charlie, while still a drunk and no good skunk according to most of the town, and according to the local police logs that I have researched over the past several weeks, well old Charlie is also known to have sticky fingers, but the local yocals just don't have enough evidence to pin on him and evidence he is accused of stealing has been fenced regionally, so there is no one around to rely on for reliable testimony.

Think old Charlie is going to get his, too, along with Schister. And my plan nabs them both. Again, the assassin from the dark side starts to rise within me. Forcefully.

Looking back once this was said and done, no one in Waseca ever found out what happened to Greg Schister a few years back. One day he was seen having coffee out at Cashwise grocery store buffet with his old high school buddy Tim Mallberg, and the next thing you know he is gone. Vanished, as if a whisper in thin air.

Up and just gone. No note, no forwarding address, food in the refrigerator and freezer but no one home to eat it. Vanished, as if a whisper in thin air.

Just gone. His vehicle was found parked in the middle of a soybean field at the Waseca Experimental Station just west of town, the old U of M Waseca campus, burned to a crisp with nothing evident except burnt metal. Not even a visible VIN.

But no Greg Schister behind the wheel. Nobody behind the wheel. And no DNA evidence available to test to see if foul play was evident. Gone…just vanished.

Well, heck…foul play was suspected, but with no body and no evidence, good luck pinning that on someone. Assassins usually win, which is why they do what they do.

Turns out old Schister was approached by old Charlie for some late night bullhead fishing out at West End Landing, (Veterans Landing today) a multi cabin site at the west edge of town that used to be run by a friend of the Rathkey family, Ted Glanton. With brother Fred living across the lake with his family on land that butted up against the Rathkey holdings, it was a nice place to relax and rest and just hang out, as an old retired guy like Ted used to do. Ah, bachelors have the life, don't they?

But with his passing years ago, the landing reverted over to new ownership that liked to keep things simple and easy going on this small, hick town of Waseca. So having access to easily accessible canoes and kayaks that just lined the south shoreline was easy pickings for a late night opportunity if one wanted to go fishing in the quiet moonlight of a late summer evening with no one being the wiser.

Old Charlie only needed the promise of a six pack and a bottle of the good stuff to entice Schister out to the landing site, and once both men were out of Schister's car and down by the lake, that bottle of chloroform would do the trick on Schister while Charlie occupied himself under the tree with his Old Milwaukee and his bottle of Jim Beam. After making sure Charlie was 'out' and the booze totally consumed did the deed reach its' time for conclusion.

Since there had to be no options for identification down the road, a quick slice from a very sharp knife severed first the left, then the right, hands from the arms. The same was done to both feet, and with Schister's body laying headfirst toward the southshore of Loon Lake, his next act as the Scot Willliam Wallace came to an end.

With what was left of the body proper, Schister was wrapped in plastic and loaded into the canoe as quietly as possible, with car keys pulled from his front pant pocket and identification removed as well. The canoe was then paddled out quietly and quickly about

75 yards on an easterly by north easterly tangent, just as I had learned.

I remember Dad telling me that back in the day, while the Minnesota DNR had begun dredging out Loon Lake for purposes of eradicating the lake of invasive fish species and milfoil invasions, the engineers had dug a 25 foot 'hole' at about this distance and dropped a 10' long by 3' in radius piece of concrete drainage tile for purposes of creating an artificial reef for future spawning and fishing development.

A few days earlier, one late evening, I had already canoed that route and place a small, fluorescent buoy marker in that exact spot, so the evening of the demise I could paddle directly to that spot, tie up the body of Schister with some old heavy chain link, and roll himself, with me, off the canoe in a free dive down to the depth of 25 feet, and place him directly within the confines of the drainage tile.

We dropped fast, as the chain did its' job in less than 5 seconds, and I only needed a few seconds to drag his body into the tile, then surface and paddle back to shore, with none being the wiser.

A body, yes. But with no hands, or feet, or head…no identification, if there would ever be a need for it. The assassin had met the challenge and vengeance was his.

I quietly brought the canoe up on shore, turned it over to drain it of the little water that had accumulated from my wet body, and went over to make sure old Charlie was still asleep under the tree.

With the amount of alcohol Charlie had inhaled…a full 6 pack and half a full bottle of Jim Beam…well, almost a full bottle…the last few ounces I spilled over his shirt with my latex gloved hand and placed the bottle down by his side. The nite was still and quiet as a cemetery. No lights visible from any of the cabins at the landing, and no activity either along the shore or on Loon Lake proper.

As we were nearing midnight, I took the gloves with me and

although I was wet, climbed into Schister's car and drove it the half mile to the middle of the soybean field at the Experimental Station lot. I pulled the gas can I had left earlier by the canoe and since then put in the car, and doused the insides and outside as completely as possible, then lit a match and took off running as fast as possible in bootied hiking shoes.

The ziplock baggies holding the last few visible remains of Schister were put in my knapsack and would be disposed of later along the way back home.

With flames starting to rise, I kept to the woods on the south side of the railroad tracks as I made my way east along Highway 14 till I was back just south of LakeShore Inn Nursing Home, where I had parked my car hours earlier. All quiet in the Nursing home lot, and the adjacent independent living apartments that were fully occupied. I stayed hidden for about 20 minutes, slipping out of my wet clothes and into a jogging suit that was in a portable bag around my back in a backpack. Wet clothes were in a plastic bag and no DNA left anywhere for anyone to suspect a thing.

I had just crossed north over Highway 14 to get in my car when I heard the first sirens of the local police, then the sheriff's department, then the fire trucks. So about 30 minutes after the fire was set it was seen and the call went in for assistance.

But the assistance would come too slowly and not in enough time, for that was not your routine, normal 87 octane gasoline that was used to light that fire. It was accelerant combined with jet fuel, which burns hotter, cleaner, and faster and leaves little to no residue in its' wake. A gift from a friend, and used exactly as described, and Bob's your uncle! I can take the container with me and dispose of along the way back home and no one will be the wiser, especially with a suspect already under suspicion.

You see, before dumping Schister over the side of the canoe, once I had him in the water I stabbed him with a hunting knife several times in both lungs, then puncturing his diaphragm and lascerating his liver and speen and both kidneys as we plunged to the lake bed. That would hasten the onset of water based scavengers to the body and help with the decomposition of the cell breakdown for purposes of possible identification…decades, at best, down the road. I knew he was already dead when I started the thrusts, but hey…I had been holding this in for decades, and I was going to enjoy it while I could.

Damn…what had I turned into that evening?

That taped knife handle held no prints and was placed next to the sleeping Charlie, and when the anonymous phone call to the police around 1 am from a burner phone indicated some unusual and possible break in activity at West End Landing, well, one can only speculate what was going to happen once Charlie was found.

I do remember reading some tidbits in the local paper now and then over the past several years as to Charlie's passing just hours after being 'found' in possession of a bloody knife that 'could not be identified' lying next to his sleeping body.

Then, again, Visine mixed with beer and whiskey can give you not only a very bad headache but one you will not regain consciousness from.

Or so I've heard.

So, in hindsight, while the reunion went well, the 'cover' of what I really needed to do in Waseca was in place and executed flawlessly. I had avenged an earlier wrong that had been done to me several decades ago. I had avenged many earlier wrongs committed by the bully Schuster to unsuspecting and very vulnerable young girls and ladies over the years…all too young and scared and feeling hopeless so that nothing reported could stick due to lack of evidence, 'he said/she said' testimony, and sometimes just lack of cooperation on the part of victims that just wanted to get on with their lives and lack of energy on the part of law enforcement to want to proceed on flimsy or non existent evidence.

But all it took, really, in the end was persistence and a drive to want to see justice done no matter what the cost.

No matter what the cost.

No matter…

Well, there might be a cost now.

As Vicki Lawrence sang…'That's the night that thc lights went out in Georgia'.

All of this information was hidden quietly for the past several years. But sometimes you need to come clean, to show up and take the fall, to be accountable for the deeds you have done no matter the who, the what, the where, the when, or the why.

All in the name of justice. I think back to the days of my grandfather, days that I was not around to see or be part of, being a Deputy Sheriff for Waseca County. And I look to the more recent past at my father, in his days as a Deputy Sheriff for Waseca County, days that I do remember and remember fondly the pride with which he served and worn his uniform and performed his duties.

How would each of them respond to me…today…knowing what I have done.

Was it done in the name of 'justice'?

Was it done in the name of 'revenge'?

Or was it done in the name of…?

It does not matter. It does not matter in what 'name' it was done.

It was done. It has been done. And to a degree, it is over, not only for me but for others.

The only question that remains now is…what happens next?

Who will determine that?

What actions will be taken?

Or forgotten?

Or forgiven?

At my present age of 71, soon to be reaching 72, the end of my journey is in sight. My tomorrows are numbered, my sunrises and sunsets will no longer be measured by what I accomplished during the day but by the few smiles I may have put on peoples' faces that day.

I am not too old to be held accountable. I have been holding my self accountable for decades, long before any one else could even spell my name, let alone see what I would become. I am my own worst enemy and my own worst critic...no one can punish me for things done in the past for I have already served my time in Hell for those things. My life has been a life of bars and restraints and conditions that most people cannot ever begin to comprehend, let alone see.

So, if the grim reaper, or the legal eagles, or the sounded horn of Gabriel should come for me, day or night, let it be with both my eyes open, both my arms open willingly to go, and with a smile that will make most people wonder what I have been up to.

My reflections on the 50 year reunion were positive and I am thankful to have been part of history for that evening. My other reflections are yet for history to judge me for. I was thankful for the opportunity, and thankful to be able to help others, not just my own selfish self.

But the story is not over. We know the facts, well, at least most of them. And we know the speculations, well, at least some of them.

But there are many others that need to hear the full story, from start to finish, so that each of them can come to their own conclusion as to what is important, what is relevant, and what is worth knowing as the future looms ahead of us.

That part of the story is still to be told, and it will be.

Just ahead...

22

RATHKEY FAMILY REUNION/ REVELATIONS

Late August, 2025
Crystal, Minnesota

It's been a month since recollecting and reconstructing those past memories and events that have since caused me to have an 'awakening' as to my true identity and heritage.

The facts, not only as I have known them through vigorous research and conversations and just plain old deductions, but also verified through an exhaustive archival search, have yielded much in the way of putting not only the past, but the present and immediate future in perspective.

The only 'problem' that still exists, as I see it, is being able to assemble my family and share with them, in a proper setting, exactly what has happened over the past almost 2 years. I want to be factually accurate, emotionally stable, and stoic in whatever their individual and collective responses will be.

That is the great unknown at this point in time: how will others react to what I have found out and if it changes 'anything' or 'anybody' in a way or manner that is other than acceptable? I don't want this information to tip any body over or to throw him or her into an uncontrollable rage over what is now to be proven as 'fact' as opposed to supposition and conjecture and theory.

Why am I so damn afraid of what others might think or how they might react?

These past two years have been almost solely focused on me, my past, my heritage and lineage, and how I will react to what was discovered. Anyone else's familial reactions will have to be considered 'secondary' or 'collateral' to the main focus of the investigations…me.

Well, if that isn't the 'high and mighty' way of laying the groundwork and setting the foundation for a family gathering! I am coming across as if I know it all, have felt it all, and will be the only one who's feelings are superior to anyone else's because it was me and me alone that instigated the original investigation, did the actual research legwork, assembled and interpreted all data and evidence found during the search, and have now constructed a framework in which to share it with my family members.

But yet, I still feel so empty and lonely, because I know that this sharing of information, no matter how 'soft' the setting or how empathetic the presentation, will be met with varied responses and reactions that I cannot control.

And there lies the crux of the dilemma!

I want to 'control' other people's reactions to what I am about to tell them, rather than just presenting the information and letting the chips fall where they may. I have no more control over their reactions than I do the rise and fall of the tides or the setting of the evening sun in the west.

I just have to let go of the 'control' feelings I have and just be honest and open and receptive to what will be their real, true feelings…just as I had to be honest and open and receptive to the information I found along the way these past few years.

My wife, Julie, is the only other person that now knows the

'full' story from start to finish, as I had to share everything from start to finish with her so she could give me a full and honest reaction to what I wanted to present to the rest of the family.

Paper files and anecdotal notes and court records don't have feelings that I need to take into consideration. Their evidence is in black and white with no connotations as to which way a person should feel. Neither do the blessed souls that came before me, and some that passed in my presence, although the secrets that were originated and kept over the years have been met by me with complete understanding and a spirit of 'thanks' for all that was done to facilitate my being here today.

So, time to get the gang together for an early Labor Day celebration before some of the grandkids are off to college for the fall semester, or high school for another year in the classroom, or to the athletic fields of their chosen sports.

Their parents will no doubt be in awe, not only of what will be told them about their ancestors, or people they thought were their biological ancestors, but also the amount and depth of information compiled to support that which is going to be told them.

But then there is also the topic of hidden financial assets that have come to bear and are in my name, in a sealed vault, in the First National Bank in Waseca. Those assets will be dispersed, first of all to the government entities that are entitled to roughly their fair share, which amounts to about 50% of the total, which by now totals well over $327,000,000 million.

Damn, son…this is going to be fun distributing and allocating that to my daughters and their children, and setting up some 'other' trust funds to be used down the road for great grandchildren and their offspring that are not even on the radar as of this family meeting. Julie and I agree that we will set up some trusts so that this 'family' money will be used wisely long after we are both gone, and that it will be kept in trust for generations to come to help each of them as they begin their lives and future endeavors.

My older siblings all had their shot at doing something of this sort during their past years when their trusts came due, so I am sure they will understand that this kid, now almost 72 years old, will have the same opportunity that they had and use the monies as he and Julie see fit, whatever those choices may turn out to be.

There is no need for me to contact 'all' other relatives, or again, those that I thought were relatives, at this point in time. Nothing productive will come from that conversation and really, when you are this close to the finish line as I am, sometimes the less one knows the better. It really won't make any difference other than satisfy some people's curiosity as to things that happened long ago.

But there is one person, in particular, that needs to be recognized here and now for sticking not only to me but with me over the years, not knowing that today was going to come but that provided support once the damn finally burst and the truth had to be researched.

To my older sister, Pauline, who, yes...is my older 'sister' in every sense of the word. Of all the other 'family' members that I identified with over the years, it was always Pauline and me that were the closest, at least over the past 50 years or so. Parents come, and then are gone. Older brothers come, some are gone while others live far away. But it was always Pauline and me that were only a phone call away, or a drive away, or a thought away.

Granted, we are not biologically related, but so what?

If it looks like a duck, and quacks like a duck, and walks like a duck...must be a duck from another flock!

Well, our flock is one in the same, always was and as we near the end, always will be.

The love of a brother for a sister, especially an older sister, is forever. Just as the love of an older sister for a younger brother, that always seemed to need her protection, her guidance, and her advice no matter how old he got. For that, I will always be grateful.

Of course, a trust fund well over $300 million goes a long way to assist in those efforts, but who's counting!

Time for a party!

The family gets together for the pre Labor Day celebration here in our Crystal home. Since it will only be a day celebration, with outside BBQ and all the fixings, people won't have to worry about staying overnight in a home that can see overnight guests on a limited basis, but not the whole damn tribe at one time.

Julie and I have not let on about the trust fund situation as of yet, and are playing those cards close to the vest so as to not give away any 'sudden wealth' acquisitions…we are still the same old Julie and Donny and will live our lives accordingly.

We may 'change' some things we do, and 'how' we do those things, but we don't want to 'change' ourselves.

Not gonna happen.

But after a stupendous and filling lunch outside, on a very nice sunny, 74 degree day in metro Minneapolis, we gather the crew together out on the patio, as Grandpa has a story to tell them and needs to have their full attention.

Funny…whenever it comes to Grandpa having to tell a story, everyone sits up straight, looks straight ahead and is paying attention. Well, as close to paying attention as one can in lounge chairs and sunglasses, with drinks in your hands and still snacking on Grandma's brownies!

Shades of my old teacher and coaching and administrator days are back in my memory banks and I love it! I say 'jump'…you say 'how high'? 😊

One hour later there is not a dry eye in the lot of them, including me. Knew I should have put out some Kleenix before I started. But the tears were not so much of anything other than joy and happiness and resolution…a secret (actually, several secrets) had been uncovered and the truths exposed, and no matter how hard one tried, the truth is the truth. It's not going to change shape or color or texture no matter how long you sit and look at it.

It remains constant.

And my family, while fully understanding not only what had happened but also perhaps why it had happened, fully accepted that which I told them, and their smiles validated that which I suspected.

Of course, individual checks in the amount of several million dollars for each of them as 'starter' funds for their various educational activities or stations in the workforce didn't hurt the morale of the day, but eh, what the heck...gotta have some fun when you can, for as far as we know, we only get to go around once in this lifetime.

As for the tail end of the story, which involved my indiscretionable behavior at West End Landing a few years back, was tempered with some updated news, which was a relief to all involved.

You see, I didn't go into specifics on the 'what' of what I did and whom I did it to, but I did allude to the 'fact' that over the past few decades, I was aware of some nefarious individuals that were involved in some very despicable activities involving assaults and hurting other women in the community, and I 'assisted' law enforcement in the apprehension of said individuals so that it would not continue into the future.

Which...to a 'degree' was the truth. I was aware, I did apprehend the individual(s), and even though one died a day later, I had assisted law enforcement so that these behaviors would not be repeated in the future by the same individuals.

Damn, son....I should have been a lawyer!

In earlier times, I might have gotten John Wilkes Booth off on a technicality years ago and probably pled out a worker comp case due to the shredding of the American flag by the stirrup on his left boot, indicating that improper attention was given to the hanging of that flag as to cause a grievous injury when Booth jumped on the stage at Ford's Theater that fateful night after his derringer accidently misfired behind the left ear of President Lincoln.

Naaaaaa... I didn't think so.

So the reveal was given, all present were accepting of what was told them, and we all parted ways later on that evening looking forward to our next get-together in a few weeks during the Archery opener for deer out in west central Minnesota home of our daughter, Tristan, and her family.

But while this story may 'seem' to be over for most people, there are still a few loose ends that need to be cleaned up and addressed by the principal involved…

Me.

23

FINAL DISPOSITION: RECONCILIATION AND DIRECTION

Waseca, Minnesota
Late fall, 2025

The air is crisp and cool this late November morning as I head south from our Crystal home, down Highway 100 and onto 494 East, and finally to Interstate 35W going south. The roads are clear, no snow as of yet, but with the temps in the low 30's it won't be long before some flakes begin to fall and Mother Nature starts to slap us upside the head and show us who really is in charge.

Julie is working on some Christmas crafting projects today, so she will not be joining me on this jaunt back to my hometown of Waseca. But deep down I think she realized that of all the trips I make to Waseca at various times of the year, this one probably should best be made by me in a solo effort. While this is a 'usual' late fall trip for me to make, this one has an additional element that needs my attention and mine alone.

My late fall, pre Thanksgiving trip includes hitting Owatonna, possibly going to their HyVee grocery store and picking up some of the mocha cakes that would rival the ones made during the days of my youth at Preuss Bakery in downtown Waseca. Rindelaub's bakery make the best glazed doughnuts and cakes, and Preuss' made the best mocha cakes and Scandinavian rolls in the region. Glad they never tried to duplicate each other…better going to see both of them!

But with both bakery's out of service and owners no longer with us, HyVee gave me my next best 'fix' so I picked up a half dozen to take back home and freeze. Well, maybe not all of them would make it home…gotta have some energy with all that driving!

Hanging a right brought me onto old Highway 14 and a 14 mile trip west to Waseca. A quick jaunt up the Maplewood Park, a brief overview of Clear Lake, then back down, past relative Kiesler's RV Campground and Barney's Drive-In brought me back to Woodville Cemetery, 'home' of many of my ancestors, as I knew them to be, but not all of them.

I drove past old markers and headstones till I reached the 'Rathkey' and then the 'Scarton' plots. Old habits died hard, and it was still within my wiring that I should continue the tradition that I had followed almost the past 50 years, that of placing late fall Christmas wreaths and spring rose arrangements just prior to Memorial Day on the graves of 'my' ancestors.

The wind seemed to be a little bit more biting as I hung the wreaths today, but it didn't take me long to attach them to the shepard hooks that I had placed there in previous outings, and after completing the same task at the Scarton headstone, I drove around the 'new' section of the cemetery to the east, looking at newer names on newer stones to see if there were any that I recognized.

Over the past few years I had gotten into the habit of at least every two months or so, checking the internet of my phone and googling 'recent obituaries' in the various towns and cities I had lived and worked in over my lifetime: Waseca, Twin Cities, Granite Falls, Ogilvie, Milaca, Aurora-Hoyt Lakes, Hibbing, Owatonna, Windom, Fairmont, Granada-Huntley-East Chain, Grove City-Atwater-Cosmos and Crystal.

Wow...that was quite a list of places we lived, both during days of professional employment and retirement. But while names will sometimes escape me, faces never do. That is one of the 'curses' of the mental talents I have with my memory abilities...things just don't seem to go away. Maybe it's not a curse, just the way I am wired.

Maybe it's time to cross wires and amp things down as I get older!

From the cemetery I would usually take a ride around Clear Lake, stop back for lunch at the old Thompson's Boat House, then move on to a quick ride around Loon Lake and then on to the new Morgan's Meats at the north end of town, so I can bring back home some goodies for my wife, Julie, and also for my sister, Pauline, who always enjoys whatever I bring back for her frig and freezer.

But today, I needed to take another jog once I got back closer to town, and was to take a turn south along Highway 13 till I got to the Dairy Queen, right across from the old Culligan Water Softner place, then take a right and go west one block, over the railroad tracks and past the old EJ Johnson electrical component factory, then hang a left and so south on the old winding road that would take me past the Catholic Cemetery a few miles out of town, and in a few more miles, pulled into the old Wilton Cemetery where several of 'my' ancestral Rathkey relatives found their final resting place.

But today was not a day to honor just those fallen souls of the Rathkey clan.

No, today I was going to start a 'new' tradition and honor the unmarked gravesite of a 16 year old girl that gave me life back on October 6, 1953...and the unnamed fetus that was mistakenly buried with her in a pauper grave, the location of such that the City of Waseca used for such entries.

A few weeks ago, on a hiatus from archery hunting after looking for my elusive whitetail deer that turned out to be not so elusive that late day in October, I spent some time at the Waseca County Courthouse Recorder's Office one afternoon between hunts on the 'old' ancestral Rathkey farmland north up in Iosco Township where I still had exclusive hunting privileges granted by cousins that owned the property. These were a few of the cousins that I had left, due to all of us being at advanced ages, so I figured no use sharing some information that may upset the old ancestral applecart, so no one was the wiser that I was not 'technically' a Rathkey anymore.

Sure felt like one....but what the heck. No use pressing my luck!

Anyway, I searched the old cemetery records for Wilton Cemetery and came across the entry for one week after my birth, dated 'October 13, 1953' in which an unnamed Jane Doe and her stillborn baby girl were interred together in the same wooden coffin and placed on a shallow grave on the southeast section of Lot 19, marker No. 4.

Well, by the time I had gotten to that spot in the cemetery, and realizing that the last time anyone probably gave credence to this exact spot was back in late 1953, there was no 'marker' to indicate anything...so I did what I thought appropriate at the time.

I had a reference point that did have a marker to the north of supposed marker No. 4 on Lot 19, so I simply deduced several 'places' to the south to account for the other graves interred around the same time and came up with the spot that I believed to be hers.

I brought with me a simple wooden cross that I had made in my garage shop, having shaped the bottom to a sharp point to allow for easier pounding into the ground, and having a 3 pound maul with me in the car, proceeded to appropriately 'mark' the previously 'unmarked' gravesite in honor of my biological mother and the born but deceased female child of my other 'mother', Irma Rathkey.

No name was inscribed on the cross, as it was never ascertained what her name was. So I scribed the word 'Mother' across the cross bars of the cross and left it at that. After pounding in the cross a good two feet into the ground, to allow for some frost heaving during the winter, I went back to the car and place the 3rd and final wreath that I had brought with me and hung it across the cross.

I am not the world's most religious man, but I do believe in a higher power and a higher authority that we all will have to answer to some day…perhaps. Or, perhaps it's all over when the lights go out and it's simple back to ashes and ashes and dust and what not.

Who knows?

But I stop and bow my head for a moment of silent reflection. Not only for what she had done and had to endure during her brief but significant 16 years on earth, but the lessons that I learned long after her passing and not at her feet, like other children.

No, the lessons I learned came from other adults that took me in, loved me as best they could, then turned me loose to fend for myself. Given the sometimes limited skills and talents in one area did not automatically atone for the sometimes gifted and somewhat outrageous skills and talents I had in other areas, but that was the way I was wired, the choices I made, and the paths I took.

I learned long ago that when life throws you a curve ball, you have only a few liminted choices to make, and you need to make it in a hurry. You can stand in at the plate, dig in your cleats, and let the damn ball hit you someplace on your body…usually in a place that is going to hurt for quite sometime.

Or, you can adjust your swing to allow for the curving arc of the ball and swing mightily at it, usually being way ahead of the pitch and screwing yourself into the batters back on the backswing.

But best yet, you loosen up your stance, loosen up the grip on the bat so it feels lighter in your hands, gauge the arc of the ball, knowing that it will break in on you, and then release your swing in one fluid motion and you watch the ball sail out of the park for a game-winning homerun....or a foul ball down the line.

Well, what did you expect? It was a curve ball, after all!

But the point is, and I thought more about this on my drive back to Waseca and my subsequent drive back to the Twin Cities...

I have made some choices in my life that I am not proud of. As a result of some of those choices, sometimes people got hurt...very hurt...or I got hurt.

I have made some choices in my life that I am very proud of. As a result of some of those choices, sometimes people were very pleased with what I had accomplished. Sometimes people were exceptionally please with what I had accomplished. And sometimes, well, usually....I was pleased with what I had accomplished.

But the bottom line was: I made choices. Good or bad, right or wrong, effective or ineffective...I made a choice.

And I again, at 72 years of age, choose to make another choice.

I choose to accept that which is given to me and laid out in front of me, no matter what the origin or the manner of source or the dialogue that accompanies it.

I choose to accept that my choices now are the most important ones in my life, what remains of it. I choose to accept moving forward that I was a flawed youth, a flawed young adult, a flawed adult, and am still a flawed old man.

This 'old enough to know better' shit had better come around soon, 'cause my days are numbered and I'd like to get it right before Gabriel calls and my time is up.

But for my family...my entire family, of which you all belong...I thank you for what you have meant to me over the years and for the good things you are doing in your lives to help make this world a little bit better place then when we each came into it.

In closing, as St. Francis of Assisi stated so many years ago...

God grant me the serenity to accept the things I cannot change.
Courage to change the things I can.
And wisdom…always…to tell the difference.

I accepted., most of the time
I had the courage, most of the time.
I tried to attain wisdom, some of the time.
What will you do?

24

ЗАКОНЧЕНО

Crystal, Oregon, Washington, DC...and elsewhere
Sometime later...

You know, most people would have been pleased to end this novel at the conclusion of the preceeding chapter. Things were discovered, resolutions made, and directions taken for the future. Maybe add a few lines in an epilogue to really 'wrap things up', but then we will come to the end…the 'real' end…of the book.

But, no….not in this case, and not with this Donny!

There is still something that bothers Donny after all these days and months of reflection, but he can't put his finger on the exact cause of his consternation. But there is something…something… that keeps eating away at the core of his being that just won't release its' grip, and it's driving him crazy.

He talks with his wife, Julie, and while empathetic to his plight and swings of emotions, there is nothing concrete that she can put her finger on to help ease the situation along. But she realizes that Donny needs to reach a higher level of acceptance to all that has taken place over the past two years, and he needs to come to grips with it quickly or things are going to go to 'Hell in a handbasket' in short order.

Finally, during the middle of a cold and blustery winter night in suburban Minneapolis, Donny wakes up, sits straight up in bed, and exclaims: 'Eureka…I have found it!'

Shades of Sherlock Holmes and Thomas Edison, and apologies to both, but that phrase would only work here!

Indeed, Donny had finally come to the realization that what had been bothering him all these past days and months was the one, single, 'loose thread' that had yet to be reconciled with. It had finally shown itself cleanly and clearly to Donny, and he now knew what had to be done to bring a 'final', final resolution to this nightmare of an existence.

Donny had yet to bring to closure the one final piece of the puzzle that as of now, had yet to be confronted:

> while Donny finally knew all that he could know about the people that were considered his 'family' here in Minnesota and the United States of America, he had yet to really discover the same about the person that brought about his existence in the first place…his biological mother and father.

All Donny knew from his past two years of research was that his mother was a 'Jane Doe', who came into 'written existence' on a ledger at the Waseca Memorial Hospital early on in the stormy morning of October 6, 1953. While unconscious in the hospital bed, she gave birth to Donny and then expired from a massive loss of blood. Nothing could be done to save her, but with the help of a very sympathetic nurse and another unsuspecting mother who had just given birth to a stillborn baby girl, the baby switch was made, the records swept 'clean', and Donny was the proud son of Leon and Irma Rathkey of Waseca, Minnesota.

Donny eventually found his biological mothers' grave out in the Wilton Cemetery and gave due credence to that new-found discovery, but other than that…that was where the trail ended, hence, that is where the story ended.

There was no place else to go.

Or…was there?

What Donny knew at the present focused on who he was and where he was, not where he had come from. And if a person really needs to bring closure to a hereditary puzzle such as this one, there has to be a committed effort to finding out all that you can not just about you but about where you really came from, assuming that those records still exist.

Well, good luck hitting the piss bucket from 3 feet with that one! When your biological mother is 'Jane Doe' and all previous records indicate as such, it was if she did not exist beyond that stormy morning and departed just as suddenly as she came in.

But there was 'another' way in which Donny might be able to help track down some more of his past genealogy, and that expert lived in Salem, Oregon and had helped Donny immensely along the path to get this far.

I wonder if she would be able to dig deeper, with multiple resources, and with newer DNA testing technology being developed every day, could help Donny finally bring the 'total' closure he so desperately needed and wanted to finally put this entire puzzle to bed…or at least bring to light all that was physically possible and leave the rest to the great unknown of the universe?

Yup…time to get ahold of cousin Desiree Spoettcher for another go around!

Within a few days, Donny had made plans to travel on the Amtrak Empire Builder, leaving St. Paul, Minnesota early in the morning and traveling west along the upper plains corridor of rails to the great Northwest, then switching trains and going south on the Pacific Coast Zephyr before taking a side trip into Salem, Oregon.

While working in both realms of public and private practice, Desiree was a foremost DNA testing expert within not only the United States but was also recognized worldwide as 'a' go-to person when you needed to find the genealogy answers you were looking for. She could work magic with her cadre of machines, testing equipment and contacts, but, again…one can only do so much with what you are given. You can't just 'invent' DNA or made some magical leap from one gnome to another…you need hard, solid evidence, and Desiree was both efficient and effective at wringing the most out of her machines and contacts to reach closure on those puzzles that crossed her desk.

Desiree had not only access to one of the premier testing labs in the world, she also had access to much of the most modern advanced testing techniques, developed in joint effort with her brother, Major Leland Spoettcher, the Agent of Charge of the Federal Bureau of Investigation (FBI) testing lab in the J Edgar Hoover Building located in Washington, DC, just blocks from the conjuncture of the White House, the Supreme Court, and the Capitol complex. His background, along with his sisters', brought a formidable team to any table when confronted with DNA puzzles; but there was still another 'bullet' to add to the cylinder to help out in this case.

While it is not common place to have such unions exist, it just so happens that Major Spoettcher's wife, DeeAnn, was the 'Agent in Charge' of the Central Intelligence Agency (CIA) DNA testing lab in nearby Quantico, Virginia, a CIA training and testing facility on the grounds of the most secure location on the face of the earth.

Well, hell's bells! There was no way that this triumvirate of knowledge and power was going to derail Donny in his quest to find the 'unknown', at least to the best of his ability.

And the time to start was now, as the Amtrak train was getting ready to leave Union Depot on its' journey west.

What made the journey west more pleasant for Donny was that many of the train personnel, all the way from engineer to conductor to brakeman to fireman to actual personnel covering the areas of loading and unloading baggage and well into the cafeteria workplaces remembered Donny from previous years.

You see, several years ago, back in the late 1990's and early 2000's, Donny was an appointed member of a national committee, the Amtrak Customer Advisory Committee, and traveled the United States FREE due to his membership on that 15 member committee. While traveling the rails and gathering objective and subjective data for the corporate offices of Amtrak, Donny became very familiar with the railroad industry and all of the obstacles that it was encountering in the legislative halls of government.

Donny's involvement as the Executive Vice President of the Committee, in his first few months on the 'job', brought him to the halls of Congress, the Oval Office of the White House, and the inner sanctum offices of the justices of the hallowed Supreme Court. Donny's testimony as to what was 'really' going on in the railroad industry, from the perspective of not only the customers but also the rail personnel, helped shape future legislation and funding priorities so that the rail system could be working in both an effective and efficient manner.

But after his initial 4 year term was over, and since reappointment to the Committee was not in the bylaws, a 'special' meeting was convened and the resulting 'Dr. Donny' Rule of Exception was unanimously adopted, allowing Donny to continue in his administrative advisory role for as long as he desired...unheard of prior to his initial appointment and rescinded after his retirement 20 years later.

But, hey...ride the horse as long as you can and then dismount before it bucks you off! It was a great ride and a great deal of bipartisan legislation was accomplished, primarily due to Donny's influence and common sense approach to solving problems, or as Donny would put it...'opportunities for advancement' with a few minor hiccups along the way.

Back to the problem at hand!

Well, the train trip was uneventful, personnel introductions made in Salem, and then on to Desiree's lab for some more informal introductions to her most modern DNA testing techniques. But this time, seeing things in person, gave Donny some more ammunition for Desiree to 'use' in helping to narrow down the quest of the hour: where did Donny's biological parents come from, or at the very least, where did his biological mother come from and if possible, where did the sperm donor hail from?

Donny was able to share some more medical information that would help Desiree narrow down, or perhaps, expand her initial search for answers to the questions that were on the table.

While it took years to develop, manifest, and become evident, it was obvious that Donny had Dupuytren's Syndrone, or also knows as 'Dupuytren's Contracture', or 'The Vikings Disease'. While the technical term in the medical field is 'Palmar Fibromatosis', the more common names work just as well.

The condition, for lack of a better word, is hereditary, which in our case was great to know. It deals with the fibrous layer of tissue that lies underneath the skin, but above the bone, tendons, blood vessels and nerves, and is located in the palm area and fingers of an individual. The fascia thickens and contracts, causing a finger or fingers to start to close toward the palm and is very painful in trying to get things to straighten out, which they won't without treatment, usually involving surgery, as the tendon needs to be severed in order for relief of pain and letting the finger relax back to a normal state of being.

This condition has also been known as 'The Scandinavian Disease' as it is exclusively known to exist only amongst those people and their descendants....which again is great for our cause. This helps narrow the potential search area for knowledge as to my hereditary origins or at least helps get me closer to the truth, whatever that may be.

Taking this new medical discovery into Desiree's lab, we begin a more thorough advanced testing process whereby we can get to the core of my issues. Any information collected will also be shared with the FBI lab in Washington, DC and the CIA lab in Quantico, Virginia…'thank you', relatives! The advanced clearance that both Leland and DeeAnn were able to gain access to for this project was immensely helpful and in the end, a real eye-opener as to what modern science can do to help track down people that need to be found, or that don't want to be found. Depends on which side of the coin you are investigating!

Well, the 'technical' aspects of this advanced testing involve knowledge and procedural application regarding the unique gene mutations and traits each of us as individuals have, including but not limited to MTHFR genes, COMT genes, CBS genes, and the MTR and MTRR gene.

Ya, I though so myself….too much information that I don't need to go into detail about, but nice to know a little bit about each of them!

Basically, Desiree and I and her team, at all three locations, will focus on the 5 fundamental steps of DNA testing, be it initial or advanced, which is what is happening in our case.

We start with sample collection (somewhat painful for this part of the process, as we are going 'deeper and wider' for the sample) and proceed immediately to DNA extraction. After some testing is completed, we proceed on to quantification and then amplification (PCR), which is just what it sounds like: we are going to enlarge and expand the sample so we have more material to include in the testing.

PCR stands for 'polymerase chain reaction' technique, which allows for the above to be testing in multiple layers and at multiple locations. We finally end with the analysis and interpretation stage, where a DNA sequence pattern can be established through capillary electrophoresis to generate a DNA profile.

And that is the profile I have travel thousands of miles to find… where did 'Jane Doe' otherwise known as my biological mother, come from? And, if possible, how about my biological father…or is that question outside of the realm of testing at this point in time?

Guess we're gonna find out…but that will take several weeks to determine, and while I love being in Salem, Oregon, I should get on home to my wife, Julie, and wait for the results to come in. I have a feeling this process is going to get quite detailed and possibly 'political' in nature, and I don't need to be around, getting in the way, during those times.

So, I say my good-byes to Desiree, on screen to the good Major in Washington, DC and to DeeAnn at CIA headquarters in Quantico, Virginia. They ensure me that this project of theirs will be given 'top' security clearance, and as only they can do, will minimize the knowledge base of anyone not directly associated with their team as this project moves forward.

I am very grateful to Desiree, not only for what she is doing for her 'cousin' but for her passion in this area of DNA testing and bringing resolution to questions such as mine. Desiree reminded me that of 'all' the cousins she has, I am the only one from Waseca that has presented her with such a challenge that she had to drop all of her other project work to concentrate on mine as it was the most puzzling she had encountered. And, having relatives in both fields of the FBI and CIA only helped add to the mystery and intrigue that we all were experiencing…it was like a damn field trip that just would not end!

But we all…me, Desiree, Leland, and DeeAnn…knew that the journey would end within a few weeks, at the latest. Or, at least, more clarity would be given at the end of their advanced testing.

You see, while Desiree could not only tell me but show me the testing materials and equipment she used for her testing process, those advanced machines and technologies in both Washington, DC and Quantico, Virginia were 'off limits' to someone with 'common knowledge' such as myself, and I fully understand why.

We are talking technology that is so far 'out there' that one cannot comprehend the awesome power that it exerts in the field if DNA testing and is something that can be used for both public and private sector usage, but also for military and black ops functions and analysis that 'John Q. Public' does not and will not know about.

So, just like eating spinach as a 4 year old, I take it, chew it, say 'thanks' and move on!

Reversing my Amtrak route to get back to Minnesota was a pleasant experience, especially when having to wait a few hours on the rail tracks due to a snowslide/avalanche in the Havre section of northern Montana. No big deal, just went to the observation car and watched the wonder of nature as a big snowblower attached to the front of another BNSF train came down the tracks and blew away the obstruction and allowed us to pass while it waited on a side railing.

Crap…wonder how much snow Julie left for me to shovel when I get home?

Well, several weeks have passed and while I waited for the 'final' results to come in from Desiree in Oregon, Leland in Washington, DC, and DeeAnn in Quantico, Virginia, I spent some time focusing on an assignment that Desiree had given me to at least 'think about' during my down time waiting.

It was Desiree's thoughts, that, based on what she already knew and what she suspected due to the additional medical information I was able to share, she had a 'hunch' on at least a general location of the possible origin of my birth mother.

Now, you have to remember we are talking over 70 years since my birth, and with a possible/probable 15-16 year old girl giving birth in Waseca, Minnesota on the stormy morning of October 6, 1953, well…that would put her birth around the late 1930's… almost 100 years ago! We already know that most United States records are skimpy, at best, at that time, especially when dealing with transcient people like 'Jane Doe' was.

But what if she wasn't from the United States?

Oh, damn…things just seemed to go from bleak to dark in a hurry. Now we are talking about international searches and miniscule documentation and…holy crap on a cracker…talk about jumping from the pan into the fire!

But, don't get ahead of yourself, Donny. Just focus on what Desiree wanted you to do and don't let your imagination run wild; at least, not yet.

The initial search that Desiree did was good information. Now we just need to trust the process and see where the new testing information leads us. Having shared with Desiree that over the course of a lifetime I have had 30 surgeries was certainly impressive to her…if for no other reason than I am a 'survivor' and a very strong constitution. That strong genetic trait may come in useful down the road as we help to identify that which is presently unknown…just gonna have to wait and see.

But the 'one' genetic, hereditary trait that I shared regarding my Dupuytren's Syndrome especially peaked her interest, and as we explored that more fully with members of her medical team, a stark discovery was made…and it may help lead us to a direction.

It seems that 'my' syndrome symptom has a unique, a very distinct, marking that is only found in central Russia. You see, in 'normal' Dupuytren's, you have a curvature upwards and inwards of the finger that is being contracted. But in my case, just under the skin level and attached to the offending tendon is 'hook' of cartilage, a small but hard piece of attached material that forms in the shape of a 'hook'.

Why?…no one in medical history knows the definitive answer. But what is documented proof is that this very unique feature is only found, and has only been found, in males of the Russian Federation from the deep taiga arboreal forests of northern, central Russia.

Well, crap....I don't know if that is good news or bad news or just news at this point in time. But it does give me pause to think about things.

But thinking in isolation can be a bad thing, as it leads to bad thoughts, and bad thoughts lead to bad actions predicated on bad decisions.

I need a drink.

But I don't drink, thanks to an Afib diagnosis several years ago. Heck, I can't even take communion wine in church once a month...I have to have the grapejuice!

OK, time for some grape juice, then. Whatever! I just need something...

Then there was a ring, and there was a phone call from Desiree.

The next hour consisted of a joint conversation between Desiree, Leland, and DeeAnn, all being able to contribute while I sat there trying to figure out if I was supposed to be crying, or laughing, or just taking it all in and leave the emotions for later.

I left the emotions for later!

I listened very intently, remembering all that I heard and from which source, and when we were finished, I looked at Julie, who was listening on speaker phone during the entire phone call. And I asked...

'Is this it'? 'Is this the end'?

Julie just looked at me, smiled, got up and gave me a kiss on the cheek like she likes to do, and simply said 'I think we have come to the end of the road, Sundance'.

(Since our favorite movie of all time was 'Butch Cassidy and the Sundance Kid', starring Paul Newman and Robert Redford, Julie and I have forever been known to each other as 'Butch' and 'Sundance', with Julie being 'Butch'...since she is the one that 'does all the thinking'!

We can discuss that preposition in another book still on the back burner! 😊

Anyway, I just sat there in a simple state of digestion and silence; I needed time to process all that I had just heard and that was best done for me laying back in my recliner, with some soft Lawrence Welk music on in the background, and just mentally drifting off, trying to put things in a framework that made some sense to me.

I trusted what Desiree, Leland, and DeeAnn said, as I knew their character was impeccable and integrity was above reproach. No, it wasn't that which I was having trouble digesting…it was the obvious:

Now that we knew the 'what' and probably the 'where', all we could do was speculate as to the 'how' and leave it at that. There were no more trails to explore, no more leads to follow, just ideas and theories and thoughts…that's all.

Let me explain.

When all was said and done, my DNA testing team did indeed believe that my biological birth mother was originally from Russia. And due to the specific genetic markers that were present in my DNA samples, while the 'exact' place of location within the Russian Federation of almost 100 years ago was impossible, the 'probable' general geographical location was an area east of the Ural Mountains, west of the Lena River, north of the Yenisey River bend (which is nw of Lake Baikal) and directly north of Mongolia by thousands of miles, it was in the ancestral arboreal forest of Siberia in an old abandoned village just south of the Arctic Circle, north of Lura.

Holy crap on a cracker! You got that all from my DNA samples? Damn, son…you guys are great!

But, I digress. Let's continue…

Due to economic declines, poor infrastructure, and a harsh climate, locales left or died there, without population replenishment, and now there are over 20,000 abandoned villages in the area known as 'Russia'. Over time, nature has reclaimed the land, vegetation has grown over old building remnants, and these 'ghost villages' exist only in memory, at best.

But it was within that geographical area mentioned above that a ghost village called 'Vladuhorst' became abandoned near the end of the 1930's, with the last single female living resident fleeing in a gypsy caravan headed to the coast and the bowels of a cargo ship headed to America.

With parents having just died from starvation, and no siblings alive to help shoulder the load and no prospects for a better life in this brutal area of the world, this young waif grabbed on to her only sighted source of refuge, and over the next several months would endure a several thousand mile journey on barren land to the coast of eastern Russia, then bound over to the crew as 'payment' for a several month ocean voyage east to the United States. The mostly scavenger Scandinavian crew was rough and demanding, but in order to live she had to get along…in whatever manner that may present herself.

Arriving in the United States via San Francisco, she would work her way east to the forested and agricultural lands of southern Minnesota, and while carrying the result of that long journey across the Pacific Ocean in her belly, found herself at the threshold of the Waseca Memorial Hospital on the stormy morning of October 6, 1953…16 years old, pregnant and ready to give birth…and unbeknownst to her, near the throes of death.

You know the rest of the story, as it has already been told. Now you know it in its' entirety.

I know nothing of my biological father and sperm donor, just that he was probably of Scandinavian descent which was left to me via some genetic mutations in the form of Dupuytren's Syndrome in my right hand. All of my 'other' dominant genetic markers are that of an eastern European/Asian ancestry which I now acknowledge with pride.

As for my biological mother…damn….what a journey!

But that also explains why I was not getting any familial hits after the DNA testing a few years back. Both parents deceased, no siblings, no supporting extended family members, and no ancestral records for documentation or comparison. It was like all traces of my ancestral background were erased and I was left…alone…by myself.

But, again, almost anyone can become a 'mother' and a 'father', and like the plaque in my office study shelf states, 'Anyone can be a father…but it takes someone special to be a Daddy'.

Yup…had that! Like I said before, Leon and Irma did the best they could with the resources and time and energies they had, and while I was not the best 'client' or 'patient' or 'son' to work on, life went on and we all did the best we could under the circumstances.

I know now more than I knew then.

And I need to remember that, no matter where I came from and from whom I was part of, it is the present with an eye to the future that demands my time and my attention and my focus for that is what is important now and will always be.

But to not only remember the past but to discover it…damn!

That was one wild ride.

But I can smell the brownies that Julie just baked, and like the good, protective husband that I am, I need to go and be in charge of quality control,

…so I gotta go!

PS---for those of you still trying to figure out the title for this chapter, '3aKOHYEHO' is Russian for 'it is finished'.

Appropriate, wouldn't you say?

MOSCOW
St. Petersburg
NORTHWESTERN
CENTRAL
Nizhny Novgorod
VOLGA
SOUTHERN
Rostov-on-Don
Samara
Yekaterinburg
URAL
Omsk
Novosibirsk
SIBERIAN
FAR EASTERN
Murmansk
Arkhangelsk
Petrozavodsk
Pskov
Veliky Novgorod
Smolensk
Tver
Vologda
Yaroslavl
Kostroma
Ivanovo
Vladimir
Syktyvkar
Kirov
Kazan
Perm
Izhevsk
Penza
Ulyanovsk
Saratov
Volgograd
Astrakhan
Ufa
Orenburg
Chelyabinsk
Kurgan
Tyumen
Salekhard
Naryan-Mar
Khanty-Mansiysk
Dudinka
Tura
Tomsk
Kemerovo
Krasnoyarsk
Barnaul
Gorno-Altaysk
Abakan
Kyzyl
Irkutsk
Ust-Ordynsky
Ulan-Ude
Chita
Aginskoye
Yakutsk
Magadan
Anadyr
Palana
Petropavlovsk Kamchatsky
Yuzhno-Sakhalinsk
Khabarovsk
Birobidzhan
Blagoveshchensk
Vladivostok
Kaliningrad
Maykop
Krasnodar
Elista
Stavropol
Pyatigorsk
Nalchik
Vladikavkaz
Grozny
Makhachkala
Kaluga
Tula
Bryansk
Oryol
Kursk
Belgorod
Lipetsk
Voronezh
Tambov
Ryazan
Saransk
Cheboksary
Yoshkar-Ola
Kudymkar

EPILOGUE

Late Fall, 2025
Crystal, Minnesota

Well, it's been almost 2 years since this horrific ancestral journey started. I am sitting back at the same computer screen that froze my thoughts and emotions in the early spring of 2024. But with a slight change…

Thanks to my wife, Julie, and family, I now am sitting in my basement office in our Crystal, Minnesota home, working off of a new hp laptop computer and accessories that my family thought I would need for the writing of this book. I had an 'older' laptop that I used for my first book, 'Stick to the Plan', published in 2015. But that only works now when plugged in to direct current; the battery is shot and to replace the battery with professional labor would be cost prohibitive. So…I gots me new equipment as a Christmas present and love it dearly. 😊

Of course, there is also a slight flip side to the deal. Having survived 30 major surgeries, including those on my ankles, lower leg, and knees…amongst other parts and joints…I don't have the best knees or hips in the world, as routine shots to both locations indicate.

Hey…I am now almost 72 so give me a break!

So, rather than running up and down stairs to access the only printer we have in my wife's upstairs crafting office, I bought her a new Epson tank printer and I got her 'old' hp that will suit my purposes just fine.

But while the physical things around me allow me to function in somewhat world of normalcy, the real question(s) at this point in time are:

… how are you doing physically?

… how are you doing mentally?

… how are you doing psychologically?

… how are you doing emotionally?

… how are you doing socially?

The answers to most of those questions is, 'I am fine', and I really am. The nightmares are less frequent now; while my weight has gone up, I am holding my own, considering my age and former athletic abilities; my mind is usually in a good place, as I tend to focus on the positive and screw everything else that I can't control; while I sometimes wear my emotions on my sleeves, depending on the situation and people around me, I am usually the 'stable' one in a setting: calm, cool, and collected.

And while I am ok around other people, I don't need to be the 'life of the party' or the 'center of attention' in a group setting. I am fine with just being myself, by myself, or in quiet time with my wife and family. I think a large part of that is my inner personality as that of a 'loner' or a 'wolf'…either that or spending too much time in my past hunting alone in a tree stand or deer blind…which is a perfectly great setting for me and my personality. Though, to be honest, I would much rather hunt with my son in law or grandsons, even if a few yards apart in different stands, but close enough to know they are there, and I am here.

But the real point of 'where are we' after all that you have read and I have gone through and now regurgitated, is:

1. Can I move on from where I was to the here and now?
2. If so, how do I do that?
3. If not, how do I overcome the barriers to that being accomplished?

Well, let's start with the obvious. Yes, I can and have moved on from the information I discovered, then uncovered, then resurrected and processed regarding several issues of my birth, my past, my existence, and my future.

I have come to realize that while my birth was not an accident (perhaps the conception was), the fact that I am alive today is the direct result of a kind and loving person taking things into her own hands to make sure that I as a baby had a fighting chance for life in a family that wanted to have another child, but due to unforeseen circumstances and of no fault of their own, had that opportunity cut short in a hospital room. Leon and Irma (well, at least Leon) knew of the situation and kept his mouth shut all these years while providing me and his wife and family opportunities for growth and development.

Why should I think that I should ask for more? Like I said…I am almost 72, have lived a long life so far and hope to keep things going as long as reasonably possible so that I can enjoy what life has to offer before my time comes.

So, yes…I have come to grips with my past…all aspects of it… and it is in the rearview mirror of my mind.

At least for the foreseeable future. Every once in a while I have to glance back to see what may be gaining on me or to keep things in perspective. But my focus is on what is here and now, and what I can reasonably plan on in the near future.

The old saying 'man makes plans and God laughs' is very true. But having a calendar on the kitchen frig that takes into consideration a full year, a month at a time, gives me hope that some plans may come to fruition while others get changed based on new circumstances.

And I also need to realize that my actions and plans are not done in isolation. There are others that need to be considered... often, consulted...before changing those plans from fast setting jello to more solid concrete. But it is those plans, and the process of making those plans, that helps keep me young and focused on a better tomorrow.

As for the second question, moving on from the past means just that: you move on. I need to move forward regardless and in spite of how I got here and what I have done in the past. It is the future that should be in my front focus, not something that I did not have any control over in the past. My conception and birth may have been accidental and then altered by circumstances, but what I did during my early, teen, young adult and older adult life years was because of choices I made and the consequences that those choices evoked.

People, especially young people, have not had enough experience yet to know that everything you do...every choice you make... has a consequence. Most of the time those choices may seem routine and second nature, with no more thought behind them than brushing your hair or feeding the dog.

You just do it.

And while most of those consequences are also inconsequential, you need to be aware of the big picture and where you fit into it. My undergrad sociology training at the University of Minnesota taught me, among other things, 'situational awareness'.

In modern speak it is used by conceal and carry firearms instructors to help make you aware of your surroundings as you and others enter into those spheres. It involves awareness skills and reactions to outside stimuli that may affect your well being and of those around you, hence the term, 'situational'. I am proud of my conceal and carry training the skills I learned that helped me not only improve my situational awareness but also help me to focus on what is important and relevant and sort out the chaff from the wheat, so to speak.

Never was a farm boy, but you get the idea!

As for the third and final question, I have moved on, so there are no barriers holding me back relative to the past.

Thoughts from time to time...yes; but not barriers that need to be addressed.

I often find myself in quiet time speed reading, a skill I learned in graduate school and that allows me to not only read but recall with perfection and clarity over 4,000 written words per minute. It only takes me less than an hour to read a 500 page novel, but I will slow down if it is a book that I 'really' want to digest and recall with absolute certainty.

This talent can sometimes impress my friends, but also piss them off! They give me a sack of books to read, as we have similar reading preferences, and I give it back to them within a few days! Life is short...read it and move on to new things!

Sitting here at the computer, coming to the close of a life-altering experience, I find myself sometimes second guessing myself as to some of the decisions I made earlier in my life. I guess that is normal to reflect back and ponder the 'what might have been'.

But I can't get myself wrapped up in those previous actions, as they are over and done with. Yes, some of those decisions have present day consequences, at least for some other people and families affected by those decisions. I am sure the extended family of Greg Schister (parents are long since dead and no siblings) and perhaps Old Charlie (turns out that was an alias!) may still carry some feelings about what happened to their 'loved' ones; now that the 'truth' has been revealed in this text, perhaps some of those feelings will surface and reignite old feuds and open fresh wounds that were once healed over. Then again, who gives a shit? Donny doesn't.

I don't know. Only time will tell. But the lines between what is truth and what is fiction, what is real and what is fake, what is authentic and what is copied…those lines are sometimes harder to distinguish and even harder to prove.

But it all comes back to this: what are you going to do about it? About anything?

I intend to move on from what I have uncovered and discovered. How I came about is of little consequence now. When you are closer to the finish line than you are the starting gate, well…your perspective can and will change about many things.

What is more important to me now is how I move forward knowing what I know, in spite of what I know, but not based on what I know.

I am still the same old Donny that I was almost 2 years ago when this 'situation' was unfolded right in front of me.

I did not ask for it, nor did I shirk away from its' possible implications. But my personality and the way I am wired made me go back in time to find out the truth, wherever that truth may lie.

And boy…did I have to dig! But I had the skills, the tenacity, and the perseverance to keep at it, no matter what. Old memories be damned…let's see where this is headed.

My sister, Pauline, told me as much when first confronted with the new found information that had been revealed to me on my computer screen. Without having the benefit of full truth and knowledge at that original conversation, she quietly told me to 'follow the evidence, wherever it may lead you and whatever you may uncover'.

That, ladies and gentlemen, boys and girls…that is true faith and courage.

The situation has been presented.

The information has led me to the past.
The past has been discovered and uncovered.
The truth has been documented and revealed.
Old memories and actions have been resurrected and confronted.
The assassin in me has been laid to rest…figuratively. Along with age-old feelings.
The information has been shared.
The manuscript has been written, the book published.
Now…now is the time for you to decide what are you going to do?
As the actor, David McCullum, as 'Dr. Donald 'Ducky' Mallard, forensic pathologist, stated on the hit tv show 'NCIS', '…we all die twice; once, when our bodies just give out, and a 2nd time, when stories about us cease to be told.'
Let my stories continue to be told…

APPENDIX A

ADDITIONAL AUTHOR'S COMMENTS

I am often asked when writing a piece of work, 'are there any 'other' thoughts or comments from other authors that help guide you along your journey'? Are there 'other' thoughts that you personally have when writing that help 'guide' you through a particularly difficult event or time while writing?

The simple answer is a quite definitive 'yes' to both questions. Let me share those with you.

'There are three reasons for becoming a writer. The first is that you need the money; the second, that you have something to say that you think the world should know; and the third is that you can't think what to do with the long winter evenings'. Quentin Crisp (1908-99) The Naked Civic Servant 1968.

This is painful. I don't even know where to begin. When I think I find a starting place, headaches, backaches, this damned cold that won't go away, all pull me down. My confidence collapses from under me and I have to curl up on my recliner until I feel better, ready for sleep. But sleep won't come.

As my sister reminds me, 'follow where the evidence leads, not where you want it to go.'

How far can a profound personal loss drive someone toward darkness? What would it take for you to kill someone, perhaps for money, perhaps for revenge, perhaps for, well, just for. And, if you did, who...or what...would you have become? These are the questions one man faced when he believes he has or will lose everyone he loves and everything he has. When the opportunity arrives to reinvent himself as a killer for pleasure and revenge, he takes it. He's good at it, and if he doesn't do it, well...but then everything changes, as he wonders if redemption rather than revenge is the dish best served cold?

The Janus Deceptions is a haunting journey though minds twisted by circumstances. A disturbing yet deeply satisfying ride... for some.

My goal as the author was to mix up the provable facts of one's person's life with facts that may or may not be fiction. I wanted to create a story, that much like quicksand, catches the reader, holds them fast, and if they struggle or if they right against suspended reality, if they even doubt the veracity of what they are reading, they will feel compelled to search for the truth; but in doing so, will only sink deeper into the novel's hold.

It is my sincere hope that someone...anyone...reading this novel will get caught up in the story and endeavor to research deeply into what is written on the pages of The Janus Deceptions, so deeply that in the end, they come to the only possible conclusions... that this novel might not be a work of fiction...that it might simply be the story of a life lived beyond what the imagination thinks can exist.

Truth? Maybe. Maybe not.

I am the only one that can tell this story. The only one alive to tell it without concern for the outcome and without regard for the results a reader may encounter.

It must be told, and it must be the truth…or as I know it to be.

'Great is the art of beginning, but greater is the art of ending'. Henry Wadsworth Longfellow

I'm ready now to do this. I'm upright at my laptop, ready to begin my story. Every time I feel overwhelmed by the desire to curl up on my recliner and pull an afghan over my head, I'll fight that urge because this is important. I just ask you as the reader to understand how hard this is. This event is so huge, it's difficult to figure out how to shrink it smaller, or even to make a start.

The definitive account, now, I cannot give to you. But I can tell you what this novel means to me. I can tell you about the research and the strategies and the mental skirmishes. About moments of trial and days of heartache. I can give you my private reflections about those, as I will do in each of the 2 Appendices.

Because that's what it all comes down to in the end. Just focus on all that is local, as all good history is personal.

Writing this novel is a selfish, lonesome thing. Going back to 1869, with stops along the way in 1909, 1915, 1935, 1937, 1941, 1947, 1953, 1955, 1959, 1963, 1965, 1966, 1971, 1972, 1975, 1996, 1998, 2021…and on and on and on up to 2025. Damn, son…that's a long journey!

But I am guided my many thoughts as this journey unfolds, the next being an overriding one. 'To the living, one owes consideration; to the dead, only the truth'. Voltaire, Lettres sur Oedipe

For those of you that think writing is only 'fun', I would add: 'A writer never has a vacation. For a writer, life consists of either writing or thinking about writing'. Eugene Ionesco

And like they say, the proof is in the pudding; or as Gilbert K. Chesterton stated…'a good novel tells us the truth about its hero, but a bad novel tells us the truth about its author.' ☺

I can only hope that if you made it this far, it's in the former category and not the latter!

When reading The Janus Deceptions, one must continually ask oneself: 'is a zebra a white animal with black stripes or a black animal with white stripes?' The answer has to be 'yes' on both accounts, for reading, as well as writing and beauty, is in the eye of the beholder. That's why The Janus Deceptions can be considered a novel of truth, interwoven with numerous threads of fiction just as well as a novel of fiction, interwoven with numerous threads of truth. It will be what you want it to be.

And you will be right.

'All writers are vain, selfish, and lazy, and at the very bottom of their motives lies a mystery. Writing a book is a long, exhausting struggle, like a long bout of some painful illness. One would never undertake such a thing if one were not driven by some demon whom one can neither resist nor understand.' George Orwell.

On the other hand, Mark Twain once wrote 'I was sorry to hear my name mentioned as one of the great authors, because they have a sad habit of dying off. Chaucer is dead, so is Milton, so is Shakespeare, and I am not feeling very well myself.'

Sarcastic bastard, isn't he?!?

I may not be deemed a great writer, as history writes my story, but I want to be great at what I did; write a fast-paced and emotionally-draining, tears on my sleeves and skin standing up on my neck personal type of adventure covering many locales over time that has a deeper meaning of what is really important in life, and wanting the reader to keep wanting to turn the page and wanting to turn the page and...you get the point!

Some may refer to The Janus Deceptions as a thriller type mystery with a lobotomy, but I don't want to fall prey to the 'you know who it is in the first chapter and now have to sit through five hundred pages of chase' formula. I want to keep you guessing well into the near end with believable characters and story lines that couldn't be described as fully fleshed out, but certainly will keep you leaping pages like a reindeer.

And with a novel that started out as a 'holy crap on a cracker' real life moment over 2 years ago, well, we've all come a long way since!

A sadistic favorite author and speaker friend of mine, Robert B. Baer, would say in his book 'The Perfect Kill: 21 laws for Assassins', 'if you can't control the kill, control the aftermath.' Well, in The Janus Deceptions, I can control the kill, but I can't control your aftermath.

But I have had to ask myself, many times, before-during-after my writing… 'can I live the rest of my life with the memories and the guilt?'

Yup. Next question.

Ursula K LeGuin is quoted as saying 'writers have to get used to launching something beautiful and watching it crash and burn.' Oh, how damn true that statement is! And how painful…

But then I turn to Jeanette Winterson who brightens up my day with 'I don't even want to please the reader…I want to change them.' Damn, girl…right on! If The Janus Deceptions doesn't reach up and grab you by the stones of Gibralter, and shake you until you're scared shitless, well, then…that's on you! I did all I can.

But I can admit that I found that the process of writing this book is very cathartic. It was painful at first, having to get up every day to relive the stress, anxiety, and exhaustion like running in a marathon. But it was worth it. The more I wrote, the more my mind became clear. And as that happened, the sense of guilt lifted.

In going through the evidence day by grueling day, I rediscovered not only the joy but the exhilaration. Being forced to reexamine those many months, years, and decades made me appreciate how hard I had to fight, against impossible odds, to elicit the truth from the pages and notes of history, but unbeknownst history to me. In the future I will want to tell my great grandchildren about this novel. And when I will be able to hand them this book and say, 'This is my story. Your great grandfather was not perfect, but he had conviction. He fought with every fiber of strength for what he thought was right.'

That's all we can ever do.

By now you will have discovered that The Janus Deceptions is a work of entertainment and should be read as nothing more, though there is fact intertwined with fiction throughout the novel. The names, characters, places and incidents portrayed in the story are the product of my imagination or have been used factiously…

Or have they?

The original manuscript was written with real people, exact geographical locations, and real time events, then re-written to extract the real personnel names and replace with fictious ones. All other locations remain as noted. Any resemblance to actual persons living or dead, businesses, companies, events, or locates is entirely coincidental…

Or is it?

Again, read the above disclaimer and then consider yourself to be forewarned.

After reading my novel!

Which bring us to a famous quote of Ernest Hemingway: 'The most essential gift for a good writer is a built-in, shockproof shit detector. This is the writer's radar and all great writers have had it.'

I am not a great writer…yet. But my shit detector is on full alert all of the time and functions 24-7 quite well, thank you very much! Your challenge, Mr. Phelps, should you decide to accept it, is: can you go back through the entire book, from cover to cover, and pick out that which is truth and that which is fiction?

Good luck with that one, Abernathy!

But to the core of this book, 'trauma splits your life into a 'before' and 'after'', as quoted on the TV series 'Chicago PD' by Sergeant Hank Voight on Oct. 16, 2024.

It is true, 'there are things that we don't want to happen but have to accept; things we don't want to know but have to learn; people we can't live without but have to let go', or so is quoted by Anonymous.

And in Macbeth perhaps it was said best…'What's done cannot be undone', (1606), Act 5, Scene 1.

So we let our conscience be our guide, so to speak. For me as an archery and firearms hunter, there is a particular virtue in wildlife ethics where a hunter ordinarily has no gallery to applaud or disapprove of his or her conduct. Whatever my actions, they are dictated by my own conscience, rather than that of onlookers. It is difficult to exaggerate the importance of that fact, and I wish I had been better in tune to it when I took a 'smaller than acceptable, but legal' deer this past hunting season, and had to share in that 'embarrasment' with my son in law and youngest grandson, both of whom took very respectable bucks within minutes of each other and an hour before I pulled my trigger. But the urge to 'contribute' overrode my good judgement to wait and hold off till later. While there was quality protein in venison to put in the freezer for my grandsons to have during their college days, and for that they were thankful, I was reminded of some words by Lucius Annaeus Seneca (c. 4 B.B. – A.D. 65), Epistles, 52, 1.12: 'You can tell the character of every man when you see how he receives praise.' I remain humble, yet hopeful, for another opportunity.

Next year I will do better, I will show more patience, more character, and be more 'Grandpa-like'.

Winston Churchill once said 'It is not enough that we do our best; sometimes we have to do what is required.' Truer words were never said, and his words helped guide me in The Janus Deceptions. I had to write things that needed to be written, dig in areas where digging needed to happen, and bring to the light of day events that had been sheltered for decades.

'The longest part of the journey is said to be the passing of the gate'. Marcus Terentius Varro (116-27 B.C.) On Agriculture (De

Re Rustica), bk, I ii, 2. Yes, that is true. That first step can either be a killer or a catapault…but it has to be taken.

'I have believed over time that some books are to be tasted, others to be swallowed, and some few to be chewed and digested; that is, some books are to be read only in parts; others to be read but not curiously; and some few to be read wholly, and with diligence and attention. Some books also may be ready by deputy, and extracts made of them by others.' Francis Bacon (1561-1644) Emblems 1635 'To The Reader'.

This certainly pertains to The Janus Deceptions. You will read it as you wish, but I caution you to absorb all that you can at the appropriate pace, lest you find yourself wondering rather than saying 'ah, haaaaa'!

Which brings us to what kind of reader are you? I agree with Goethe: 'there are three kinds of readers: one, who enjoys without judging; a think, who judges without enjoying; another in the middle, who judges while enjoying and enjoys while judging. The last class truly reproduces a work of art anew; its members are not numerous. Johann Wolfgang von Goethe (1749-1832): letter to Johann F. Richlitz, June 13, 1819.

For those of you that are more 'nerdy' than you want to admit or to have others know, when you get around to including DNA in any type of writing, you must remember that 'DNA neither cares nor knows. DNA just is. And we dance to its music.' Richard Dawkins.

Such is true of the ABO system used in The Janus Deceptions. This is the best known method for the classification of blood, which was divided into four types: A, B, AB, and O. Eighty-five percent of the U.S. population is either type A or type O; 10 percent is type B, and only 5 percent is AB. A concomitant classification method called the Rhesus system further divides the four types into Rh positive or Rh negative, depending on the type of Thesus antigen present in the red cells. Eighty-five percent of all blood is Rh positive. In other words, I know that finding someone with AB-negative blood was a major pain in the ass. But since the Abo system has only been in existence since the 1930's, I know there was no practical way of testing the notion, since I did not have actual historical fluids to work with during my periods of research.

In closing, I would like the reader to know two additional points. The first is that I, and others, came up with over 60 different possible titles for this novel, settling on The Janus Deceptions since there is significant 'two-faced' ness in this novel, and severe levels of deception in all decades of research. Plus, the play on words with my wife's name was priceless!

But I also have this 'draw' to want to bring attention to my hometown of Waseca, Minnesota, and the part it plays in my novel. 'The Waseca Enigma' remains in the forefront of the back of my mind...perhaps it will be resurrected down the road in some fashion...as it brings attention to and a curiosity to the role of the many locales in a great hometown.

We'll see!

Those other titles are still 'in the wind' and on the drawing board, so to speak, and I may be at the mercy of my agent, editor, or publisher to change my choice before the final printing. But that is a decision for another day.

To my sister, Pat, who urged me to follow the evidence, print the truth, and seek peace in my heart...before she realized that fiction and fact can be inextricably linked. Damn, that was a nice Clear Lake walleye that just took this idea 'hook, line, and sinker'...☺

And to my wonderful children: Kristin and JJ, and Sarah, and grandchildren Hayden, Logan, Brody, Brett, and Reese. My wish for you is to honor the past and your history and those who came before you. Cherish the present and embrace it, as these moments, once presented to us, are gone forever. And be brave, not only in your attempts and intentions but your results. Have faith in your

future, respect yourselves, and always be true to yourself, kind to others, and true to your soulmates. I love you....Dad/Grandpa
PS---I hope the royalties will be put to good use, as it is my desire that they are coming your way.

APPENDIX B

ADDITIONAL NOTES, QUOTES, AND TIDBITS

In the same vein as Appendix A, but on a different track, I am often confronted with periods of quietness and peace when other thoughts come into my psyche and play around with what I am trying to write. It does not distract me, but it does give me pause, and I reflect on these extraneous interruptions as 'being there for a reason'. What that reason is, I have no idea. But it works! These can also be 'jumping off points' for the start of a new book or perhaps a hidden book title, perhaps one of yours, or mine. Let's find out together!

I share those notes, quotes, and tidbits with you now. Authors noted when verified and appropriate.

> 'Thinking is the hardest work there is, which is the probable reason why so few engage in it.' Henry Ford (1863-1947) inventor of the moving assembly line.

If you ask the wrong question, you'll never get the right answers.

'Better to write for yourself and have no public, than to write for the public and have no self'. Cyril Connolly (1903-1974): in New Statesman Feb. 25, 1933

Be prepared to go where the evidence takes you, even if it takes you somewhere you don't want to go.

'The world may be full of fourth-rate writers but it's also full of fourth-rate readers'. Stan Barstow (1928-: in Daily Mail Aug. 15, 1989

Be tenacious as hell with a chip on your shoulder.

There but for the Grace of God go I. On, wait…I did go there!

'A book is a mirror; if an ape looks into it, an apostle is hardly likely to look out'. Georg Christoph Lichtenberg (1742-1799): Aphorisms

To everyone who's faced their worst nightmare and come out stronger on the other side, this book is for you!

0 + 0 = 0.

'Difficulties mastered are opportunities won'. Winston Churchill

Shit sandwiches don't taste too good, and are even harder to swallow.

'It's not so much what you believe, it's how hard you believe it'. Harrison Ford in 'TJ and The Dial of Destiny', 2023

'Cover up' or 'covered up'?

Standing on dignity or falling on your sword?

Extrapolate emotional responses, predict possible thoughts, analyze the past, evaluate the present, and predict the future.

There's only one way to eat an elephant…one bite at a time.

Is this a serious undertaking, or am I just pissing into the wind?

'I want to tear myself from this place, from this reality, rise up like a cloud and float away, melt into this humid summer night and dissolve somewhere far, over the hills. But I am here, my legs blocks of concrete, my lungs empty of air, my throat burning. There will be no floating away'. Khaled Hosseini, 'The Kite Runner'

Open the door. Turn on the light. Walk ahead.

Does this change me? Who I am? What I am? Where I came from? Where I am going? What I am going to do?

I' did not know it was possible to be so miserable and live but I am told that this is a common experience'. Evelyn Waugh, letter to Harold Acton, 1929.

'Get busy living or get busy dying'. (Morgan Freeman in the movie 'Shawshank Redemption')

Excuse me for finding out who I really am.

'What matters most is how well you walk through the fire'. Charles Bukowski, 'how is your heart?'

Everybody is somebody…or are they?

Flip a coin: heads or tails?

'Courage is what it takes to stand up and speak; courage is also what it takes to sit down and listen'. Winston Churchill

What now?

'I don't know Who…or what…put the question, I don't know when it was put. I don't even remember answering. But at some moment I did answer 'yes' to Someone…or Something…and from that hour I was certain that existence is meaningful and that, therefore, my life, in self-surrender, had a goal'. Dag Hammarskjold, 'Markings'

Genealogy secrets.

'Never take advice from someone who doesn't have to live with the consequences'. Mark Cuban, owner of the Dallas Mavericks

Older doubts.

'No one can make you feel inferior without your consent'. Eleanor Roosevelt

Sleuthing

'Thou canst not think worse of me that I do of myself'. Robert Burton

Face to Face…to a fault.

'The world breaks everyone and afterward many are strong

at the broken places'. Ernest Hemingway, in 'A Farewell to Arms'

It was a dark day. But faith works best in the dark.

Love doesn't lie.

'My pencils outlast their erasers'. Vladimir Nabokov

The Siren of Trust and Curiosity.

'A lie gets halfway around the world before the truth has a chance to get its pants on'. Winston Churchill

Did I lose something…or did I find something?

These are the masters. Learn from them, be inspired by them, and though you may never pass through the Asgardian gates and take your place among them, you will be better for having known them. Anonymous

Foundations of sand make for slippery slopes down the road.

Anger or contrition?

'Be open to change: just because it's typed on your lovely computer it doesn't mean it's any good'. Tracy Chevalier

Dead bodies must remain dead.

Am I a better man, or a bitter man?

Dig deeper or skim the surface.

Is it too late to start this life over?

She really didn't know…or did she?

We all have secrets. Some poorly kept.

Trying to hit a moving target, while moving.

Now I understand.

Tomorrow.

'One should look long and carefully at oneself before one considers judging others'. Moliere (1622-73): Le Misanthrope 1666

Who in their right mind climbs headfirst into a 70 year old rabbit hole?

Hope can never be 'Plan A'.

If at first you don't succeed, don't consider suicide.

OMG…now what?

When you're closer to the finish line, your perspective changes.

Stop me if you've heard this one…

Where there's smoke, there's fire.

Prayer only works for the faithful.

Have my eyes changed, or my heart, or my head?

Be glad you're you.

Am I less or more, for undertaking that quest?

2-4-6-8, who can I just blame and hate?

DNA does not lie.

Why didn't I know?

Secret liasons seldom remain as such.

'One writes only half the book; the other half is with the reader'. Joseph Conrad (1857-1924): letter to Cunninghame Graham, 1897.

We put some dark in, only so our light will show. You have to have dark in order to show light.

'Life isn't about waiting for the storm to pass. It's about learning to dance in the rain'. Unknown

'The wise man draws more advantage from his enemies that a fool from his friends'. Thomas Fuller

'God grant me the serenity to accept the things I cannot change; Courage to change the things I can; and wisdom… always…to know the difference. St. Francis of Assisi

As the saying goes, you can sometimes talk to 'crazy' but there's no dealing with 'stupid'.

Twisted Redemption…has a foreboding ring to it, doesn't it?

'The only way I can tell that a new idea is really important is the feeling of terror that seizes me'. James Franck, Nobel Prize winning physicist.

Be careful sliding down the razon blade of life.

'A professional writer is an amateur who didn't quit'. Richard Bach

'The road to ignorance is paved with good editors'. George Bernard Shaw

'Kill your darlings, kill your darlings, even when it breaks your egocentric little scribbler's heart, kill your darlings'. Stephen King

'Publish only to satisfy our craving for fame; there's no other motive except the even baser one of making money'. Thomas Bernhard

'You can't judge a book by its cover but you can sure sell a bunch of books if you have a good one'. Jayce O'Neal

'I get up in the morning, torture a typewriter until it screams, then stop'. Clarence Budington Kelland

'The book trade invented literary prizes to stimulate sales, not to reward merit'. Michael Moorcock

'Poets can survive everything but a misprint'. Oscar Wilde

The light at the end of the tunnel IS a train, you damn fool!

Resolution and Re-dedication…which one comes first?

'The most valuable of all talents is that of never using two words when one will do'. Thomas Jefferson

'Confidence is going after Moby Dick in a rowboat and taking the tartar sauce with you'. Zig Ziglar

'A young musician plays scales in his room and only bores

his family. A beginning writer, on the other hand, sometimes has the misfortune of getting into print'. Marguerite Yourcenar

You're not your circumstances. You are what you make of it.

'I heard that Amazon has started a program to try to get people to trade in their old bound books to get an electronic reader. They call it 'Kindling'. Kate Deimling

'Easy writing makes hard reading'. Ernest Hemingway

'Writing is a place where you can lose your innocence without losing your virginity'. Germaine Greer

'This is one of those cases in which the imagination is baffled by the facts'. Winston Churchill, on Rudolf Hess, a prominent Nazi, parachuting into Scotland.

'I am irritated by my own writing. I am like a violinist whose ear is true, but whose fingers refuse to reproduce precisely the sound he hears within'. Gustave Flaubert

'My wife joined a book club. They primarily read wine labels'. Unknown

'Don't be dismayed by the opinions of editors, or critics. They are only the traffic cops of the arts'. Gene Fowler

'I thought to myself, why not write a best seller? In the first place, more people read them, you make more money, and it doesn't take anymore time to write a bestseller than it does to write a book that nobody buys'. George Burns, from 'The Third Time Around'.

'Nothing, not love, not greed, not passion or hatred, is stronger that a writer's need to change another writer's copy.' Arthur Evans

'This must be a gift book. That is to say a book, which you wouldn't take on any other terms'. Dorothy Parker

'Draw your chair up close to the edge of the precipice and I'll tell you a story'. F. Scott Fitzgerald

'You just can't write and write and put things in a drawer. They wither without the warm sun on someone else's appreciation.' Anne Morrow Lindbergh

'A good speech should be like a woman's skirt: long enough to cover the subject and short enough to create interest'. Winston Churchill

The more my head screams, the bigger the monster lying in wait. The monster must be released, subdued, free, silenced, and…?

'We all want things we can't have. Being a decent human being is accepting that.' John Fowler, 'The Collector'

'And remember, you must never, under any circumstances, despair. To hope and to act, these are out duties in misfortune'. Boris Pasternak, 'Dr. Zhivago'

'It is not the critic who counts; not the man who points out how the strong man stumbles…the credit belongs to the man who is actually in the arena, whose face is marred by dust and sweat and blood; who strives valiantly; who errs, who comes up short again and again…but who does actually strive to do the deeds; who shows great enthusiasms, the great devotions; who spends himself in a worthy cause; who at the best knows in the end the triumph of high achievement, and who at the worst, if he fails, at least fails while daring greatly.' Theodore Roosevelt, 1910

' How often we recall, with regret, that Napoleon once shot at a magazine editor and missed him and killed a publisher. But we remember with charity, that his intentions were good.' Mark Twain

'Finishing a book is just like you took a child out in the backyard and shot it'. Truman Capote

'There is nothing to writing. All you do is sit down at a typewriter and bleed.' Ernest Hemingway

'Most of the basic material a writer works with is acquired before the age of fifteen.' Willa Cather.

'Writing a book is an adventure. To begin with, it is a toy and an amusement; then it becomes a mistress, and then it becomes a master, and then a tyrant. The last phase is that…you kill the monster, and fling him out to the public'. Winston Churchill

'Truth has been the object of my search, and I am not conscious of ever having turned aside in my enquiries from any fear of the conclusions to which they might lead. Charles Babbage (1791-1871) inventor of the locomotive pilot

'That's the way it is with most mysteries. There are always more questions than answers. Few things wrap up nice and tight like they do in dime store novels. That's probably why I like reading them so much. I hope you find it interesting or at least not terribly boring.' Anonymous

'Very few of us are what we seem to be'. Agatha Christie, 'The Man in the Mist'.

'Every good story begins with a good question'. Helina Reijn, Director, 'Babygirl'

The above notes, quotes, and tidbits settle me down, keep me focused, and keep me going in times of question, times of despair, times of questioning…which is pretty much all of the time when writing a mystery novel. There is always 'another' way to approach anything…but is it the 'right' way for my novel? Which is why when striving to be a better writer, one needs to be a better reader. 😊

ACKNOWLEDGMENTS

It is with a sincere sense of gratitude and admiration that I pay tribute to those that were an inspiration to me not only in the formative stages of bringing this book to fruition but also in the 'process' of bring it alive…from ideas to written drafts to final editing and thus the final product you now hold in your hands. To list you all would mean that somebody may have been left out, and that is unacceptable. So I give a heart felt 'thank you' to one and to all… here's hoping that I still have another one in me to write down the road! If not, then I hang my hat on this one and be content.

But in honest reflection, there are several people that deserve to be mentioned, and as primary author, it is my prerogative to do so here.

To our good family friends, Tom and Susan Boettcher. You were the 1st ones to give me an audience when this idea was still in its' infancy. Thank you from the bottom of my heart for your honest reaction to what I hoped was going to be a dream fulfilled…getting you to bite 'hook, line, and sinker' on that plot was awesome! And it was fun!!! We still have many books to read, to share, and good times to experience down the road. Take care of yourselves so we can all do it together.

To my entire nuclear family: wife, Janis; daughters Kristin (JJ) and Sarah; grandchildren Hayden, Logan, Brody, Brett, and Reese; siblings Pat and Jerry. To you comes the real challenge: you get to figure out who the 'real' characters are in this book and separate fact from fiction when it comes to script. It was fun writing the 1st draft using real names and places and events, for what is easier to remember than the truth? Then, going back and changing those names to 'protect' the integrity of those that are living along with those that have passed...that was a real hoot! Oh, the first replacement names that were originally thought of would have our parents spinning in their graves! Come to think of it, the ones I used might have the same result! Oh, well...maybe I'll get it right in the next novel!

To my older sister, Pat, with whom I played a terrible trick but needed your honest response to the possibility of writing this book in the first place. Your immediate reaction to the original plot was priceless...your honest reaction was 'follow the evidence' and 'do what you have to do'. And I did. We did. Thank you!

In that same light, to our older brother, Jerry...I purposely did not tell you about the writing of this book for fear you may try to talk me out of it! But I hope you are as proud of the final product as I have been of you all my life. You were always the 'rock'...not the kind that drags you down but the kind that keeps things steady and on course. Thank you!

To Mom and Dad...you did your best with what you had been given. Talent, resources, and patience are not always given out in equal measures to each of us. As for me, I ran the gauntlet of all your skill levels: a challenging young boy, sometimes eager to please but usually coming up short; a terror when it came to imagination yet grounded in knowing right from wrong, if only for a short period to time; a young man stiving to fill the shoes of siblings that were an inspiration to not only our family but to others; an adult trying to walk the straight and narrow, only to find out that the wire is sometimes too thin and not strong enough to hold both me and my demons; and finally a grandparent getting older but trying to stay young enough to contribute to those I leave in my wake. I look at our daughters, their families, and know that while the name 'Bathke' is coming to a close at the end of this particular branch of the family tree, the roots and off-shoots are strong from what it has produced. The future is bright and in good hands. My blood still runs through the veins of those that not only walk the earth now but in the future…that is a life well lived.

And many thanks to Mark Dupaul, Senior Consultant and Lori Conser, Senior Project Manager and her team from Wheatmark, Inc. for making this dream become a reality. This publishing company certainly leads the rest of the pack.

Dutch N. Almasboi is the pseudonym used by Waseca native and published author Dr. Jon E. Bathke (*Stick to the Plan*, 2015) and 'Grandpa Jon's Hunting Journals, Volume I, II, and III'…99 stories from childhood thru the present that share the joy, excitement, and disappointment of experiencing nature in the woods and lakes of Waseca, the state of Minnesota, and other great states and nations. The son of Leonard ('Dutch') and Alma Bathke, life-long but since departed residents of Waseca; Jon grew up in simpler times, with simpler pleasures and simpler decisions. But his parents and siblings instilled in him a drive for educational excellence and attainment…always striving for that next degree, that next promotion, that next…you get the idea! His early professional foundation as a high school social studies teacher and football, wrestling, and track coach grounded him well, as did later administrative positions as assistant principal, principal, assistant superintendent and superintendent. Add to that positions as an adjunct professor in Educational Administration at the University of Minnesota-Duluth and working for a local, metropolitan, wealthy Minnesota family as their Vice President, Jon rounded out his professional life with a wealth of experience balanced against the values of growing up in a rural, southern Minnesota community where 'family' mattered more than the size of your wallet or the reach of your ego.

Dutch can be reached at j_bathke@msn.com.

Made in the USA
Monee, IL
30 November 2025

36892070R00152